WAR
WOMEN

Martin Limón

Copyright © 2021 by Martin Limón

Published by
Soho Press, Inc.
227 W 17th Street
New York, NY 10011

Library of Congress Cataloging-in-Publication Data

Names: Limón, Martin, 1948– author.
Title: War women / Martin Limón.
Description: New York, NY : Soho Crime, [2021]
Series: The Sergeants Sueño and Bascom novels ; 14
Identifiers: LCCN 2021027163

ISBN 978-1-64129-279-5
eISBN 978-1-64129-280-1

Subjects: GSAFD: Mystery fiction.
Classification: LCC PS3562.I465 W363 2021
DDC 813'.54—dc23
LC record available at https://lccn.loc.gov/2021027163

Interior design by Janine Agro, Soho Press, Inc.

Printed in the United States of America

10 9 8 7 6 5 4 3 2 1

To Ernie Cassell

WAR WOMEN

–1–

Strange wasn't in the Snack Bar.

Most mornings he sat at his usual table, sipping on a cup of hot chocolate, perusing the Pacific edition of the *Stars & Stripes*. By 0730 hours, he'd hoist himself upright, stick his folded newspaper into his back pocket, and mosey on over to the 8th Army Headquarters building, about two blocks away. There he'd let himself into the steel-reinforced Classified Documents vault, hang up his hat and his jacket, roll open the iron-barred customer window, and start handing out reports stamped CONFIDENTIAL or SECRET or, upon occasion, TOP SECRET. After, that is, the supplicants presented their military identification and properly annotated the sign-out/sign-in register with the date, time, document number, destination, and purpose of acquisition.

But this morning, for some reason, he wasn't at his usual table in the big Quonset hut that housed the 8th Army Snack Bar.

I don't think Ernie noticed. He hurried to the serving line and ordered a bacon, lettuce, and tomato sandwich. Because my stomach was gurgling, I grabbed an overpriced fruit cup out of the display cooler. After a quick stop at the cash register, we walked toward the rear of the Quonset hut, a few people nodding to us along the way.

Ernie was just slightly over six feet tall with a pointed nose and green eyes peeking accusingly out at the world from behind round-lensed glasses. Not particularly good-looking, I thought, but for some reason—a reason unfathomable to me—women found him attractive. Maybe it was his energy; a nervous compulsion to "fire them up." That is, cause trouble.

I was a couple inches taller than Ernie, maybe twenty pounds heavier. On the darker side. Hispanic. The gringo stereotype of a mugger. Together we made people nervous, which more often than not was the desired effect.

At the back wall, we found an open table, plopped porcelain mugs onto Formica, sat down, and began discussing the day's work.

"More black-market detail," I said.

"Riley's got a hair up his butt," Ernie told me.

He was referring to Staff Sergeant Riley, NCO-in-charge of the Administrative Section of the CID Detachment; a stickler for keeping tabs on the black-market arrest statistics. His boss—and our boss—Colonel Walter P. Brace, the 8th Army Provost Marshal, briefed the 8th Army Chief of Staff at least twice weekly on our so-called progress on the black-market detail. In other words, on how many *yobos*—the Korean wives of US servicemen—we'd busted buying duty-free PX and commissary goods on the American compound and selling them for a nice markup.

The Korean War had been an era of death, pestilence, and starvation. Now, two decades later, the standard of living was improving, but not by much. The black market was an income flow that often meant the difference between a Korean woman's extended family being fed and having a roof over their heads, and being thrown into the street. Sometimes it paid for a younger sibling's tuition so they could attend high school and thereby land steady work in the viciously competitive Korean job market. So Ernie and I didn't feel great about busting people who were just trying to keep their family afloat.

"Our black-market stats must be low," I said.

"The lowest."

"Screw 'em," I told Ernie.

He agreed wholeheartedly.

We arrived in the CID office just prior to the ceremonial firing of the 0800 start-of-business cannon. I'd just sat down at the wooden field table that served as my desk when the phone rang. Miss Kim, the gorgeous and genteel admin secretary, picked it up and identified herself. Then, in a sweet voice, she said, "Just a moment, please," and covered the receiver with her palm. "Georgie," she said, holding out the phone. "For you."

I walked over, took the phone out of her hand, and said, "Sueño here."

"Agent George Sueño?"

"That's me."

"I'm Specialist Orting, over at the Eighth Army head shed."

"Yeah?"

"You probably saw me a few times. I work for Sergeant Harvey."

For a moment I wondered who he was talking about, and then it came to me. The man we called Strange was actually Sergeant First Class Cecil B. Harvey, a senior NCO who was only two stripes below the pinnacle of the enlisted rank hierarchy.

"Okay," I said. "I remember you, Orting. What is it?"

"It's about Sergeant Harvey. He isn't here."

"Maybe he's just late."

"Him? Never. He always arrives at least a half-hour early."

Orting was right. A man's work can become his life. Like breathing. It even has a similar rhythm. The good air comes in and the bad air goes out, endlessly, in a reassuring pattern. Work is like that. You crawl out of bed on a Monday morning, drag yourself through the day, then bless your lucky stars when it's finally time to get off and go home. After a few hours of rest, you wake up and start the whole process again. The cyclical routine, punctuated artfully by weekends and holidays, has a salutary effect. God is in His heaven, a four-star general is in command of the 8th United States Army, and all is right with the world.

This pattern is especially appreciated by non-commissioned officers. They don't call us "the backbone of the army" for nothing. We're the ones who are there in the morning, taking roll call, making sure all the doors are open, the lights are turned on, and the operation keeps humming during the workday. And then, at close of business, we make sure everything is secure and turned off, and another successful day is properly recorded in the annals of military history. NCOs, people like Strange, are the men who kept the army breathing.

"Why are you calling me?" I asked Orting.

"I don't want to tell Major Cranston. Not yet. He's our OIC." Officer-in-charge. "I'm hoping Sergeant Harvey just overslept or something."

"You don't want to get him in trouble."

"Exactly." Orting seemed relieved that I understood. "Besides, Sergeant Harvey told me that if anything ever went seriously wrong, I should call you."

"Me?"

"Yes."

"He gave you my number?"

"Yes. Criminal Investigation Division. Eighth Army. He made sure I wrote it down."

This was sort of a compliment, I supposed. Although Strange had his differences with Ernie and me, he knew we wouldn't bail on him. At least he hoped we wouldn't.

"What's Sergeant Harvey's quarters address?"

"Senior NCO billet 332, Room 7."

I wrote it down. "North Post?" I asked.

Yongsan Garrison, the 8th Army headquarters compound, was divided into North Post and South Post. South Post was mostly dedicated to officer quarters and housing for the few dependent families who were allowed in Korea.

"I guess," Orting replied.

"You haven't been there?"

"Nobody has. Sergeant Harvey mostly keeps to himself."

"Like a hermit."

"You could say that. He attends the office parties, but he always comes late, sits by himself, and leaves early."

"He keeps a low profile," I said.

"The lowest."

That sounded like Strange, I thought. Waiting for everyone to get half-soused, listening to their loose lips as they sank a few ships. Mentally recording the data, then slipping out when no one was looking. That was his value to us. Not only did he control classified documents, but he was a notorious gossip— or more precisely, a collector of gossip—and his information had proven invaluable to us in more than one investigation. He wasn't supposed to pass any classified info on to us—in fact, it was illegal. Ernie and I didn't officially have a need-to-know. But more than once, these illicit revelations had helped us crack a case wide open and even saved lives.

The quid pro quo was that every time we saw him, he led with the same question: "Had any *strange* lately?" And either Ernie or I, usually Ernie, had to come up with a satisfying answer. Ernie would tell him some story about his latest sexual conquest, and, meanwhile, I'd go to the serving line, draw Strange a fresh cup of hot chocolate—with *two* marshmallows and a stirring spoon—and serve it to him, and in return we'd receive our information. It made us feel soiled, but so far, all his information had been accurate and well worth the extra hot shower or two.

"Okay," I told Orting. "I'll go check on Sergeant Harvey."

"*Great*. I gotta go. People waiting at the window."

"Go ahead."

He hung up. I lowered the receiver and turned to Ernie.

"What?" he said.

"Hat up," I told him.

He walked over to the coat rack and slipped on his fatigue cap. Thirty seconds later, we were outside in the jeep, Ernie firing it up, revving the engine, and slamming it into reverse.

"What's wrong with the old pervert?" Ernie asked.

He drove uphill toward a row of Senior NCO billets near a cement-walled three-story building formerly known as

KMAG, Korean Military Advisory Group. They'd become famous at the start of the Korean War. In June of 1950, the North Korean People's Army, led by the Communist dictator Kim Il-sung, crossed the 38th Parallel and invaded South Korea. The officers and men of KMAG, who'd been living the cushy life of advising the South Korean Army, suddenly found themselves in the middle of a combat zone. They burned their classified documents and left Seoul, fleeing south from the onslaught of the advancing Communist forces. Dodging snipers and enemy fighter planes, they eventually made their way to the American-controlled Pusan Perimeter, some two hundred miles south of here; at least, those who survived did.

"There it is," I said, pointing toward the right. "Building 332."

Ernie pulled over and turned off the jeep. We climbed out, entered the side door of the single-story quarters building, and wandered down a thinly carpeted hallway. At the end, we turned left until we found Room 7.

"Strange," I shouted. "It's us. Wake the hell up!" I pounded on the door.

Across the hallway, in Room 6, a man peeped his head out the door. "What the *shit*? Some of us work nights, you know."

"Where's Sergeant Harvey?" Ernie asked, motioning toward Strange's room.

"If it were my week to watch him, I'd know."

"You want us to break the door down?" Ernie asked.

"Please don't," the man said wearily.

"So who has a key?"

"Check with Kimmy Ajjima. She's probably in the kitchen, or the washroom."

He shut the door, and Ernie ran off to find her. I waited patiently, wondering what the hell could be wrong with Strange. We'd never known him to be much of a drinker, nor into drugs. I figured he either wasn't here, or worse, we'd find him lying in bed, not breathing, killed by a life's worth of overindulgence in cup after cup of hot chocolate with two marshmallows.

Ernie and the woman I presumed to be Kimmy Ajjima approached from down the hallway. She carried a load of olive-drab underwear in her arms. Being housemaid to a building full of GI slobs meant that she couldn't afford to waste a trip. She hugged the stack of T-shirts and boxer shorts as she stared up at me.

"Sergeant Harvey," I said. "*Odi gasso?*" Where'd he go?

"He go workey," she said definitively.

"Did you see?" I asked, pointing toward both my eyes.

She shook her head negatively. "Not my business."

"Then how do you know he went to work?"

"He *all the time* go work."

I motioned toward the door. "Open, please."

She frowned and handed the stack of clothes to Ernie. In the military, there was no prohibition against unreasonable search and seizure, and everyone knew it, including Korean housemaids. This housing unit, along with almost everything in it, belonged to the US government, and privacy was one of the many things you surrendered when you raised your right hand and took the oath of enlistment. Jangling a bunch of keys, Kimmy Ajjima stepped forward and deftly popped open the door.

It was dark inside. I felt around for a switch and found it, and an overhead fluorescent light buzzed to life. Ernie handed the laundry back to Kimmy Ajjima. She grabbed it and darted off down the hallway.

To my relief, the bed was empty. The room was pristine, everything neatly arranged: combat boots, low quarters, and civilian shoes lined up in the closet as if prepared for military inspection. The bed was carefully made with the edge of a crisp white sheet folded over a dark-green army blanket. A row of books sat on a shelf. I expected them to be dirty, a banned-in-Boston type of thing, but they were mostly nonfiction reads about psychology.

Ernie followed me in, picked up one of the books, and riffled through the pages. "Figures," he said.

"What?"

"A pervert like Strange would wanna know what kind of nut job he really is."

I ignored him and checked the field gear. Steel pot, web gear, rain poncho, canteen, ammo pouches—all present and accounted for. A leather toiletry case sat on a shelf next to a small percolator. The percolator was cold, no used grounds inside, and the toiletry case seemed to have everything the well-groomed GI could hope for, including a straight razor, nail clippers, and dental floss. A half-empty bottle of PX-purchased mouthwash glistened blue in the fluorescent glow.

"Judging by this room," Ernie said, "you could say two things about Strange. First, he's a neat freak."

"With the help of a full-time maid."

Ernie nodded. "Also, he doesn't live here."

Ernie was right. The wastebaskets were empty. There was nothing like an open bottle of bourbon or a case of beer or a hot plate with scattered Samyang ramen wrappers that one would find in most GI barracks.

"And not a girlie magazine in sight," Ernie said.

Hands on his hips, Ernie studied the room. Finally, I said what I assumed we were both thinking. "So maybe he lives in the ville."

"Ville" was GI slang for village. That is, one of the bar and nightclub districts that sprang up like weeds right out-side of US military compounds. In these parts, the nearest GI ville would be Itaewon, the red-light district at the southern reaches of Seoul.

"Maybe he's got a *yobo*," Ernie said.

"Or something," I replied.

I returned to the hallway and chased after the still-busy

Kimmy Ajjima. She was folding more laundry and with the back of her hand wiped a wisp of gray hair from her forehead. I asked her where Sergeant Harvey lived off post.

"How I know?" she asked, exasperated.

"Does he have a girlfriend?"

She waved her hand dismissively. "Not my business."

"You must've seen something about where Sergeant Harvey is living."

She thought about it. "Like what?"

"I don't know. Like maybe a bill from a *yoguan*." A Korean inn. "Or a receipt from a store or a restaurant."

"Receipt?" she asked.

"*Yongsujeung*," I told her.

"*Yongsujeung?*" She looked flabbergasted. Korean businesses didn't use cash registers much—probably because they couldn't afford them—and written receipts were rare. "No," she said. "No have."

"Did he ever show you a photograph? Or say something about a woman or a friend?"

"Sergeant Harvey? He don't have friend. I think he no have woman."

"What makes you say that?"

"Never, you know, catch *itchy itchy*." She mimed scratching her crotch.

"The crabs?"

"Yeah. Never have."

She oughta know, washing his laundry every day.

I figured I'd reached a dead-end but took one more shot. "So you have no idea where Sergeant Harvey goes every night?"

"Sure, I know where he go every night."

I paused, debating my next question. This woman was cagey, answering only precisely what was asked and thereby keeping her nose out of the complicated machinations of GI business. Finally, I said, "How do you know?"

"He tell me."

"So where does he go?"

"He go see North Korean, he tell me. Listen to radio talk about Kim Il-sung."

I held my breath. This wasn't what I'd expected. Some sort of sexual deviancy, yes—that would've made sense. But this? I tried not to show my surprise.

The Communist regime of North Korea broadcast propaganda every evening on a frequency that was strong enough to traverse the thirty-five miles from the DMZ to Seoul. Technically, it was illegal for South Korean citizens to listen to the program, but clandestinely, people did. Mostly for laughs. To marvel at the outlandish claims that the North Koreans made. For example, that the Great Leader, Chairman Kim, was a direct descendent of Dangun, the divine founder of the Korean race. And that the people in the south were enslaved under the boot of ruthless American imperialists, who were raping their women and robbing their country of its wealth.

Well, some of their propaganda rang true.

I composed myself and turned back to Kimmy Ajjima. "Sergeant Harvey knows somebody from North Korea," I said, "and he listens to the radio with them?"

She nodded.

"Why?"

"How I know?"

"Is this person a spy?"

"A what?"

I didn't know the Korean word. "You know," I said, "like *kong kong chil.*" Double O Seven.

"No. No spy."

"Then what?"

She said a Korean word that I didn't understand, but I pulled out my notebook and had her write it down. She frowned at the task, and after looking at her childlike *hangul* script, I realized why. She was old enough to have been educated during the Japanese occupation, a time when only Japanese was taught in school and a student could be punished for speaking Korean. As such, her literacy in her native language was limited.

I thanked her, bowing and tucking the notebook in my pocket.

Back at Strange's room, Ernie locked the door and we returned to the jeep. On the drive back to the CID office, Ernie asked, "What'd you find out?"

"That Strange has been listening to North Korean propaganda."

"*Whoa!* That doesn't sound like him. He's a rabid right-winger."

"Maybe. Or maybe that's just an act."

"Doesn't seem like it."

"No, it doesn't." More than once, Strange had harangued us about traitors and Commies in the US government, so passionate about the subject that spittle had erupted from his thin lips. Neither Ernie nor I agreed with a word of it, but we didn't interrupt, because occasionally at the end of his lecture—or the end of his cup of hot chocolate—he granted us a nugget of information that was pure gold.

When we returned to the office, I borrowed Miss Kim's Korean-English dictionary and looked up the word Kimmy Ajjima had written down for me: *talbugja*. The English translation: defector.

-2-

I called Specialist Orting and let him know that Sergeant Harvey wasn't in his quarters. Riley had already contacted the 121st Evacuation Hospital and determined that Strange hadn't been checked in there. Miss Kim, meanwhile, was busy calling Korean hospitals, but so far, there was no word of any unidentified foreigners being admitted.

"He's probably okay," I told Orting. "Do you have any idea if he has a *yobo* off post or goes somewhere else regularly?"

"No. He never mentioned anything."

Just then, a gruff voice barked through the receiver, as if someone had snatched the phone from Specialist Orting.

"This is Major Cranston. Who am I speaking to?"

I identified myself.

"When you find that jerk-off," Cranston said, "tell him he'd better get his fat ass in gear and get to work pronto, or he'll be facing an Article 15—maybe even a court-martial."

"I'll be sure to let him know, sir."

"You do that!"

Cranston slammed the phone down. So much for inter-departmental cooperation.

"So what do we do?" Ernie asked.

"No leads," I said. "The only thing I can think of is to alert the MPs. Put an APB out for him."

"That'll make him officially absent-without-leave," Ernie said.

"No choice," I replied. "Cranston already knows. Also, we should alert the KNPs." The Korean National Police. "If that doesn't work, tonight we make our usual rounds out in Itaewon and hope he contacts us."

"That'll be difficult."

"Yeah," I agreed. "Barrooms and nightclubs. Tough duty."

That evening, a hostess named Miss Pei clung to Ernie's shoulder, staring up at him dreamily. "Why you don't take Miss Pei home tonight? Most tick payday. Pretty soon you have *taaksan* money."

"I'm a poor boy," Ernie replied.

She pinched a button on his sports shirt. "You GI. Not poor boy."

She had a point. Most Korean families, the lucky ones, were getting by on the salary of a single wage-earner. Usually the father's. Teachers and policemen and firemen considered themselves lucky if they cleared the equivalent of a hundred and fifty dollars per month. With that, they paid rent, tuition for the kids—if they stayed in school beyond the sixth grade—food, clothing, and electricity. And during the long Korean winters, they had to purchase charcoal briquettes to fuel the *ondol* gas flues that ran beneath their floors. After all those expenditures, most families had nothing left. Not even a thousand *won*—about two bucks—of disposable income.

An American GI, on the other hand—somebody who was more often than not a knuckleheaded teenager—made the same salary every month, even if he goofed off on the job. And most, if not all, of his pay was disposable income—a GI's housing in the barracks was free, including utilities and heat. He was provided free medical and dental care. In the army chow hall, also gratis, he was served three hot meals a day. And he even had clothing provided. An initial issue of four sets of fatigues and a dress green uniform with one jacket and two pairs of pants, plus three types of headgear, two types of footgear, and a dozen or so sets of socks and underwear. If he decided to buy civilian clothes in the PX or in the tailor shops outside the military base, that was up to him. So with approximately a hundred and fifty crisply minted US dollars in his possession each month, the young American GI was a man amongst men. A boulevardier. A big spender.

And where did most of the young GIs stationed on Yongsan Compound spend their money? In the bars and nightclubs and brothels of the nearby ville of Itaewon.

It was a place Ernie and I knew well. Because this was where a GI with a snootful of booze or a head full of marijuana smoke would sometimes rob a Korean cab driver or mug a fellow soldier in a dark alley or beat up a Korean business girl who refused to do everything he wanted her to do. In other words, it was a haven for debauchery—and a haven for crime.

Itaewon was our beat, our home. Ernie and I knew every dark alley, every hole-in-the-wall soju house, and every bar or nightclub that had ever switched on a glimmering paean to gaudiness. We were kings of the Itaewon night. Vicars of the booze and the broads and the barbarism. Or at least that's how we thought of ourselves. To the reprobate GIs and most of the bartenders and waitresses and business girls, we were probably nothing more than cops. Another pair of MPs or KNPs or ROK Army *honbyong* or curfew-enforcement police sent to patrol their domain at all hours of the day and night.

Ernie and I sat in the King Club, on the main drag of Itaewon, sipping from frosted brown bottles of OB Beer.

"Maybe we should go to a joint that's more out of the way," Ernie said.

"I want to make it easy for Strange to find us."

"Yeah, but this place might be *too* easy. Too many nosy Eighth Army GIs, too many business girls, too many curious eyeballs."

"Maybe you're right," I said.

We glugged down the last dregs of our suds, set the bottles down, and paraded out the King Club's big double doors.

For a moment we stood on the broad steps, peering up and down the neon-spangled lane. Kimchi cabs—boxy four-door sedans—lined the roadway, ready to whisk GIs back to the compound or anywhere else in this vast metropolis of Seoul they decided to go. Business girls in form-fitting shorts and halter tops tottered up and down the cobbled road in six-inch heels. Canvas-covered carts offered deep-fried potatoes and yams and onion rings, just the right snack for half-looped GIs with a hankering for terminal heartburn.

Ernie and I wore our running-the-ville outfits. Sneakers, blue jeans, sports shirts with buttoned-down collars, all of it overlaid with nylon jackets sporting embroidered fire-breathing dragons on the back, his wrapped around a voluptuous Asian siren. The lettering below mine said: *Republic of Korea, 1970 to 1975*. Ernie's said: *Frozen Chosun, I've Served My Time in Hell.*

He was a sucker for the dramatic.

Occasionally, in the sparkling distance, a whoop of joy lifted above the milling crowd.

"Paradise," Ernie whispered, and I think he believed it. We stood a little longer, hoping that either Strange or someone he'd sent would be lurking in the shadowed lanes, watching us; waiting for their chance to make contact.

Ernie snapped his fingers. "There's one place Strange mentioned."

"What's that?" I asked.

"I should've known." He turned to me. "Remember that day in the Snack Bar not too long ago, when he was going on and on about how the country's gone to hell and the Koreans aren't obedient anymore because there's too much industry springing up and they don't have to rely on Americans for steady employment anymore?"

"Who could forget?" I said. It was a gross exaggeration. Most Koreans were still struggling to get by, but there was no way to convince Strange of that.

"He mentioned that guy he talked to," Ernie continued. "The Korean guy who owns a restaurant or something. 'Arrogant' is the word Strange used. Said the Koreans were becoming 'arrogant.'"

"Yeah, he said he was a *halaboji* with a nice outfit and an imported Japanese wristwatch. Not a peasant in hemp cloth, which pissed him off."

A *halaboji*, or grandfather, often wore *hanbok*, traditional Korean clothing, which included loose white cotton pantaloons with a tunic made of the same material and covered with a blue- or jade-colored vest.

"What was the name of that place?" Ernie asked. "Strange said it was on the edge of Itaewon, away from where GIs usually drink."

"I don't remember," I replied. "But I do remember that the name of the joint wasn't in English."

"Which pissed him off even more. But that also means that somebody took him there—somebody who could read the sign."

"A local. Or at least someone who could speak Korean," I said.

"Right."

"Why didn't we ask him more questions about the place?"

"Because it was just more of his blather. You changed the subject and finally coaxed him to cough up the info about that field grade officer who was selling copper wire."

"Yes," I said. "But what else did he say? Wasn't it something about the menu?"

Ernie's mouth crinkled. "That obnoxious shit."

"What obnoxious shit?"

"You know. Raw octopus. Still wriggling."

"*Nakji*," I told him.

"If you say so."

A species of miniature, long-armed octopus was often considered a delicacy in the Far East. It was served raw, its tentacles continuing to wriggle, even after being cut off, due to posthumous nerve activity.

"Why would Strange be at a place like that?" Ernie asked.

"Whoever he was with must've coerced him. Dragged him inside."

"Who could coerce Strange?"

Ernie and I looked at each other. Strange was known to be unbelievably stubborn, but we were learning so much more about him. Including the fact that he apparently had some sort of relationship with a North Korean defector.

A little girl holding a cardboard container filled with various types of chewing gum bowed in front of us and tried to convince us to buy a pack in a sing-song voice. Ernie pulled a shiny hundred *won* coin out of his pocket, asked her if she had any ginseng gum, and when she said no, handed her the coin anyway and shooed her away.

"So who could lead Strange around by the nose?" I asked. It was a rhetorical question, but Ernie came up with an answer.

"Someone with a good story to tell."

"Story?"

"Yeah. About getting some *strange.*"

We made a circuit around the village of Itaewon. After covering about 180 degrees, we stopped to rest.

"You been reading all the signs?" Ernie asked.

"Every one. No *nakji* yet."

Ernie crinkled his lips again. "How can people eat that stuff?"

"Pure protein," I said.

"Have you eaten it?"

"I poked it with my chopsticks once, just to make sure it wasn't alive. It wasn't."

"But it had been, up until just before that."

"Fresh fish," I replied. "What's the difference if you kill it and freeze it for six months? It's still dead."

"There's such a thing as a mourning period."

"You're just squeamish," I said. "We kill living things to eat them. Same difference if we committed the evil deed two minutes or a week ago."

"I'll stick with pork chops," Ernie replied. "At least pigs don't have tentacles."

On this side of the village, vehicular traffic was almost nonexistent because the lanes were poorly lit and too narrow for easy passage. We traipsed through them, occasionally getting a slightly startled stare because GIs seldom came back here. There were small open-fronted *kagei*s, convenience stores selling cold soda and puffed rice discs and dried cuttlefish. We also passed a few mom-and-pop *yakbang*s, pharmacies that dispensed not only drugs but also inexpert medical advice; stationery stores that specialized in texts and notebooks required at the local public schools, rice wine stalls with cheap cuttings of pork sizzling on open-air braziers; and repair shops of every kind: bicycles, shoes, windows, locks, and even an herbalist shop with an acupuncture operation upstairs.

Dozens of additional signs stretched down the lane, some in neon, some hand-painted, all in either *hangul* script or *hanmun*, Chinese characters.

"Can you read all that shit?" Ernie asked, gesturing to the row of glimmering advertisements arrayed before us.

"Sure. Some of it I don't understand, but if I see someone selling *nakji* or any other kind of seafood, I'll know."

"From the smell?"

"From that and the radical."

"The what?"

"The Chinese radical. A lot of characters have pictographs in them that mean things like water or wood or fire or earth— or even fish."

"You're shitting me."

"I wouldn't dream of it," I replied.

"How do you know this stuff?"

I shrugged. "Night classes."

"I thought you were through with those."

"I am. I took all the Korean-language classes they had on base. Now I study on my own."

"How?"

I gestured toward the array of advertisements surrounding us. "By reading these things, looking up what I don't know, talking to people."

"Christ, Sueño, you're too damn smart for the army."

"The honchos don't seem to think so."

"They just hate to admit that an enlisted man knows any- thing they don't." Ernie grabbed my arm and stopped me. "Wait. You missed something."

"What?"

"An entire alley." He pointed. "There. On the right. You were looking to the left."

"Okay, I missed it. Because you were gabbing too much."

"Me?"

We backed up and Ernie pointed once again. The pathway was lined with dirty brick on one side and wooden walls on the other; completely deserted, except for a small plastic sign illuminated by a single bulb.

"What's it say?" Ernie asked.

"Are you able to read it?"

"Hell, no. That's why I asked you."

"Good thing you stopped me. That's what we're looking for."

"Nakji?"

"You got it."

"See? I'm not as dumb as I look."

"That might not be possible."

As we entered the lane single file, me leading the way, we saw a metal pole canted slightly to its left with a white placard on it. Stenciled on the sign in black English lettering, it said: OFF-LIMITS TO US FORCES PERSONNEL. NO ADMITTANCE.

Many of the poorer areas on the outskirts of Itaewon had been placed off-limits by the honchos of 8th Army. Sometimes, it was because of lack of sanitation and the risk of catching a communicable disease. Other times, it was because it had been designated as a high-crime area. Often, it was both.

Ernie and I breezed past the sign. As far as I knew, nobody ever paid any attention to them.

Ahead, just past the *nakji* sign, something moved. A shadow. A man's, I thought, moving away from us. And then another. It emerged from the opposite wall, going in the same direction. The two phantoms followed the curvature of the pathway and were soon swallowed by the night.

It was a tiny joint, just a hole in the wall. Both Ernie and I had to duck in order to navigate through the front door without bumping our foreheads.

Three Korean men sat at rickety wooden tables. They stared up at us listlessly, and two of them turned back to shoveling noodles into their mouths. Apparently, raw octopus wasn't the only thing they served here. On the wall was a menu printed on a large whiteboard. I spotted *ojing-eo*, squid, next to the character for noodles.

Behind a splintery wooden counter an old woman sat slouched on a stool. She wore both a stained white apron and a white bandana tied around black hair. I put both hands on the counter, leaned forward, and asked her, "*Yogi ei nakji issoyo?*" Do you have octopus here?

"*Isso,*" she replied. We have. Her eyes widened a little at the request.

I showed her my badge.

Two of the men behind me sensed what was going on. They both lifted their porcelain bowls, hurriedly slurped down the last of the broth, and, wiping their lips with the backs of their hands, exited the tiny restaurant. Only one man was left. Older, wearing traditional Korean pantaloons and a tunic and blue vest. He hadn't been eating but rather seemed to be making entries into a ledger with a small brush and a bottle of black ink. He'd stopped, curious about what was going on.

"I have an American friend," I told her, speaking Korean. "He came in here once and ate *nakji*. Do you know him?"

I expected that even one American coming into this rundown little joint would be a novelty. She stared at me dumbly. Surprised, apparently, that I spoke Korean. Her mouth opened slightly, but before I could repeat the question, the man at the table spoke up.

"I know," he said in English. "Stupid man."

I turned to him. "Maybe stupid," I said. With both hands I mimed a mask across my eyes. "He always wears dark glasses."

"Yes." The man nodded, pointing at his lips. "And something for his cigarette."

Strange wore sunglasses regardless of whether it was night or day, and habitually had a plastic cigarette holder between his lips. To my knowledge, no one had ever seen him smoke, although he insisted that he was trying to quit.

"Yes, him," I said. "Do you know where I can find him?"

The man shrugged, holding up his palms. "In his home."

I noticed his watch was a recent Seiko model, just as Strange had described.

"And where is his home?" I asked.

"Are you police?"

"Yes," I replied.

"Is that American man, the one with the dark glasses, is he in trouble?"

Actually, Strange *was* in a heap of trouble. Being absent-without-leave for an entire day would almost certainly result in Article 15 non-judicial punishment. Less than a court-martial but still serious. With a stain like that on his personnel record, it would be almost impossible to be promoted another stripe to master sergeant. There was even a chance that he could be denied reenlistment, which would mean he wouldn't be able to serve the minimum twenty years required to put in for retirement. That translated into the loss of a monthly retirement check equivalent to half of his active-duty pay for the rest of his life. Not to mention the loss of all medical benefits for himself and a spouse, if he ever found one. In other words, tens of thousands of dollars' worth of governmental benefits could fly out the window like an escaped canary; all because he missed a day's work.

I shrugged. "Maybe a little trouble."

The man thought about it and then said, "I will write down for you."

He ripped a piece of paper from a pad, grabbed his writing brush, dipped it in ink and started stroking long lines.

I glanced at Ernie. He stood near the entranceway, arms crossed, face impassive, except he raised one eyebrow as if to say, *What in the hell have we got here?*

A woman walked in and, upon seeing us, was startled at

first, but still went to place an order with the older woman behind the counter. Within seconds, chopped squid tentacles were tossed into boiling oil and began to sizzle.

Metal clinked on metal. A faint sound, as if coming from behind a wall. I looked around, wondering if Ernie had heard it, but judging by the bored look on his face, he hadn't.

As the man sketched, he continued to speak in English. "He very stupid man. Say Korea will always be poor because Koreans always fight each other. And cheat each other. I told him that soon—maybe ten years, maybe twenty—we will be rich country. As rich as Japan."

"He didn't think so?"

"No. He think Koreans stupid."

After that remark, I allowed a little time to pass. The man worked away industriously, and from my vantage point, I could see that he was drawing a map. Apparently he was almost finished, because he was writing in annotations now.

I decided to push for more information. "When he came here, did he eat *nakji*?"

"No way."

"Then why did he come?"

"His girlfriend. She eat *nakji*. He pay, then he sit and watch."

Girlfriend? Strange? That was red-letter news.

"She stupid too," the man said.

"Why do you say that?"

"Because she's beautiful. Why would a Korean woman like her spend time with a fat man like him?"

The squid tentacles were done, and the cook scooped them in batches out of the hot oil, allowed them to drip dry for a few seconds, and ladled them atop a mat of layered newspaper. When all the tentacles were neatly piled, she folded the paper deftly and shoved the greasy package into a plastic bag. Money was exchanged, and the woman who'd gotten the squid pushed through the front door, probably on her way home to feed her family.

Now the clinking was easier to hear. Definitely metal on metal, coming from somewhere downstairs. I thought I recognized a pattern to it, but then abruptly, it stopped. Maybe just old pipes, I thought, or somebody doing some sort of repair job.

Finished with his artwork, the man in the *halaboji* outfit stood and handed me the map.

As he pointed out a few things, I asked, "How do you know where he lives?"

"This area, everybody know where everybody live. This house," he said, pointing at our destination, "is famous."

"Why?"

"Famous for Kwon Halmoni." Grandmother Kwon. "She take care of three grandchildren."

I thanked him for the map, folded it, then slipped it into my pocket. "But a grandmother taking care of grandchildren, that's normal, isn't it? There must be plenty of grandmothers doing the same thing. So why is Kwon Halmoni famous?"

His eyes widened. "Because she's from North Korea," he told me. "She escaped."

"Escaped?" I said, surprised. "With her grandchildren?"

"Yes. And her beautiful daughter."

"And this beautiful daughter, she's the American man's girlfriend?"

He nodded. And then he surprised me with his English acumen.

"Believe me," he said, "she could do better."

-3-

The map was precise.

A block and a half down, we passed Queen Min's Laundry, and at the next crossing lane, we turned left at the local charcoal distribution yard. A dim patch of light shone in the yard—apparently, someone was working late. Wheeled carts were lined up and loaded with cylindrical charcoal briquettes; ready, I supposed, for delivery first thing tomorrow morning. After passing the yard, we took the first right, and our destination was the third house on the left. The gate was open, and a yellow glow poured out.

We pushed through the old wooden planks, an ancient hinge groaning under weather-beaten weight. Across a flagstone courtyard, an oil-papered door had been slid off its runners, the latticework frame canted precariously off-center. Inside, a naked bulb burned. Bathed in its harsh glow, an old woman and three children crouched on the vinyl-covered floor—the boy about ten, a girl maybe three years younger, and a toddler playing with an overturned plastic cup. They wore the expressions I'd seen too many times. Shock mingled with fear and a growing apprehension about what would happen next. The toddler was the only one in the group who appeared not to have a care in the world.

The old woman stared at us, her face blank, expecting nothing good. We stood outside in the courtyard, not stepping up onto the narrow wooden porch.

"*Halmoni*," I said. Grandmother. "*Wein ili heissoyo?*" What happened?

She looked away. "He's not here," she said in Korean.

"Who?"

"*Abboji*," she said. "*Migun abboji.*" The GI father.

I was pretty sure she was talking about Strange, but to confirm, I said, "The guy with the dark glasses?"

She nodded.

"Where did he go?"

Her shoulders tightened. She hunched forward and stared at the floor more intently. I said again, "Where did he go? Did he go with someone?"

The woman remained immobile and stared at the floor, refusing to speak.

The boy mumbled something. He too was staring at the floor. Then I realized what he had said. "*Nabbun nom.*" The bad guys.

"What bad guys?"

No answer. Neither the old woman nor the young boy said anything.

"How many were there?" I asked.

Again, no answer.

Finally, tentatively, the little girl raised two fingers, like Winston Churchill's V for Victory sign. Then she looked to her grandmother, then to me. "Mother doesn't like them."

"Be *quiet*," her grandmother told her without looking up.

The little girl lowered her head.

The one-room hooch was mostly bare, just some old, tattered sleeping mats, a few blankets, and a plastic armoire in the corner. Sitting atop a short folding-leg table sat a framed eight-by-ten photograph. A woman stared evenly at the camera. She was young, maybe thirty or a little older, with long black hair that reached below her shoulders. Her eyes seemed wise, confident, older somehow than the smooth complexion of her skin. Her face was long, almost rectangular, and beneath a fairly prominent but round-tipped nose was a pair of full, sensual lips. Half smiling, like a Korean Mona Lisa, she seemed ready to take on the world, her preparations secret, known only to herself.

The little girl noticed me staring at the picture.

"*Urri ei ohmma*," she said. Our mother. When I didn't respond, she added, "*Yeppeu ji?*" Isn't she pretty?

I broke my gaze from the beautiful woman and turned to Ernie to translate. "They say he's gone."

"I can see that."

"But she won't tell me where he went or who he went with."

Ernie studied the frightened little family. "If we're planning to beat the information out of them, I'll let you handle it."

"No need for that," I said. "When we were at the *nakji* place, did you hear any weird sounds?"

"Like octopi pleading for mercy?"

"No. Like old pipes. Or metal clanging on metal."

Ernie thought about it. "Maybe something. Couldn't make it out, though."

"But you sensed that there was something to be made out," I said.

Ernie thought about it again. "I guess I did."

"And I saw two shadows earlier."

"What shadows?"

"When we first walked into this neighborhood. They were watching the area. Saw us coming, going into the *nakji* restaurant."

"Okay," Ernie said. "Clearly they're scared. Somebody's watching the neighborhood. We heard weird sounds at the restaurant. What does that add up to?"

"It adds up to we go back there and search."

"Okay," Ernie agreed. "But ask her one more time if she knows where Strange has gone off to."

I did. But the old woman remained perfectly silent.

Something *thumped*.

Ernie and I turned our eyes toward the back of the hooch. The old woman and the boy were still looking at the ground, and the toddler lay on his side, as if about to go to sleep. The only bit of motion I detected came from the little girl's eyes, which darted back and forth between us and the sound out back.

Then we heard a thump again, louder this time.

I nodded toward Ernie and he started toward the rear of the hooch. I followed.

Most of these multiple dwelling compounds had wooden outhouses behind them, maybe two or three, and a narrow passageway between the back wall and the surrounding fence. We knew because Ernie and I had searched more than a few of them. This place was a little different. There was only one outhouse, a permanent structure made of cement blocks. Ernie peeked inside, searched with his flashlight, then turned to me and shook his head. There was space to the left, behind the hooches, but also a passageway to the right behind what appeared to be a small storage room.

Neither Ernie nor I were armed. Checking .45s out of the Military Police Arms Room was a hassle. We had to sign the weapon out, plus the ammunition and the shoulder holster, and when it was time to turn it back in, we were required to break down the pistol, clean it with wire brushes, dip each part in solvent, wipe the entire apparatus off, and then rub the moving parts with a light coating of oil to avoid rust. All this even if we hadn't fired it. As a result, we often didn't bother checking out firearms. Besides, there was total gun control in Korea. The only people authorized to utilize a firearm were military or law enforcement. Criminals caught with guns were dealt with harshly and usually faced long prison terms, so most of them, even the organized mobsters, stuck with traditional standbys: clubs, knives, axes, iron sickles, hammers, saps, cudgels, lead pipes. Just the basics.

All Ernie and I had at the moment was our bare hands.

The sound had come from our right. Ernie headed toward the back of the rickety wooden storage room. I was just about to station myself in the front when I heard footsteps approach from behind. I crouched. Good thing I did, because the business end of a shovel whooshed through the air and clanged loudly against a wooden post. The front door of the storage room burst open, and three people emerged in a tight jumble.

Whoever had swung the shovel had recovered and was now using it as if it were a blade, jabbing at my face and toward my stomach. With my bare hands, I warded off the sharp metal edge as best I could, but in trying to dodge the onslaught, I lost my balance and tumbled backward.

Ernie rounded the corner behind the storeroom, but just before he reached me, the guy with the shovel swung it full force at him and caught him coming in. Ernie grunted and bent over, but his sacrifice gave me the opening I needed. I hopped to my feet, grabbed the guy from behind, and slammed him to the ground. As he lay there groaning, I ripped the shovel from his hands and went after the other guys, using the shovel as the army had taught me in bayonet training.

By now, Ernie had recovered and found some sort of stick, maybe a broom handle, and used it to slash at the remaining thugs. We were holding them off pretty well, but one of them had a knife, a switchblade open and jabbing, and the other two were using lead pipes.

Ernie and I backed across the courtyard and finally reached the front wall and the small open doorway that led to the street.

"You go through first," Ernie said.

"No, you first," I answered. "This shovel's longer than your broom handle."

He didn't argue. He turned and quickly ducked through the door.

I jabbed at the closest thug one last time, and then, without turning around, backed through the small enclosure. Ernie was prepared to run, but I motioned for him to wait.

He stared at me quizzically but soon understood what I was up to.

When the first thug peeked his head through the doorway, I slammed him with the flat end of the metal shovel. He howled and backed up quickly, then I dropped the shovel and we took off running.

"That oughta slow them down a little," I said.

"Not much," Ernie replied.

We sprinted back the way we had come, but within a few seconds, footsteps pounded behind us.

"We gotta do something," Ernie replied.

We rounded the corner at the charcoal distribution point, and an idea dawned on me. I burst into the entranceway, grabbed the metal handle of one of the wooden carts, and jerked it out onto the narrow road.

"Get another!" I shouted at Ernie.

He did.

Just at the corner, out of sight from someone approaching, I turned the cart over and poured the briquettes out onto dirty blacktop. Ernie did the same, creating a minefield of bowling-ball-sized cylinders from one side of the narrow road to the other.

We left the carts where they were and took off running again.

A block and a half later we approached the now-dim sign ahead that said *nakji*.

"Over here," I shouted, and we darted around a corner. Hidden by a stone wall, we crouched and looked back at our little barrier of cylindrical charcoal briquettes. It worked better than we had hoped. Apparently, at least one of the thugs had stepped on the charcoal, slipped, and was now being helped to his feet by a fellow thug. The third was cussing out both of them.

As we stepped away from the corner, I spotted a crack behind the buildings lining the road, including the *nakji* house, and another cement-block wall. To call it an alley would've been generous. It was barely wide enough for a man to wedge himself through sideways. In the distance, a street-lamp shone from the main drag about fifty yards ahead, but as dim as that was, it still revealed a network of spiderwebs guarding the passageway.

"In there?" Ernie asked.

"Yeah," I replied. "It should lead all the way to the back of the *nakji* house."

"Christ. If you say so. At least those thugs won't follow us. Unless they love spiders."

"They'll figure we headed toward the safety of the main drag. Plenty of people there. Witnesses. Maybe even a KNP patrol."

"Yeah. Who in their right mind would head down this passage to hell?" He stepped toward the crack. "It'd be nice if I had something to ward off these creepy crawlies. Maybe some soju."

"They won't hurt you."

"Says who? Some of them might be poisonous."

"Don't worry, we have full medical."

"There's a load off."

Ernie twisted his shoulders at an angle and sidled into the narrow opening. I followed. About twenty yards in, the crack widened enough to walk normally. Garbage cans lined the back walls, and when the reek of rotting fish began to over-power us, we knew we'd arrived at the *nakji* house. We paused at the back door. I checked the handle. Locked. I leaned in and listened. No clang of metal on metal.

"Maybe they repaired the plumbing," Ernie said.

"No. After we left, I think the guy who drew the map was busy contacting those thugs and ordering them to find us."

"Why? What were they trying to do? Besides kill us, I mean."

"They probably weren't planning to kill us."

"Could've fooled me."

"Just beat us up. Scare us a little."

"You can't be sure it was him who gave the order," Ernie said. "But it might have something to do with Strange going missing."

"It might."

As if someone had heard us talking, the metal-on-metal ticking started again. I leaned my ear up against the wall and listened. Finally, I backed away.

"No doubt," I said.

"No doubt about what?" Ernie asked.

"Morse code."

"Christ, Sueño. You know Morse code?"

"Learned it when I was a Woodcraft Ranger."

"What the hell's that?"

"A youth group. Like the Boy Scouts."

"You? A Boy Scout? Chicanos do that?"

"Why not?"

His face twisted in disgust. "It figures you'd be into something wholesome."

"I've forgotten most of what I learned, but that's pretty basic. The universal call for help."

"What do you mean?"

"I mean *dot-dot-dot, dash-dash-dash, dot-dot-dot.*"

"And that is?"

"SOS."

"Like what they serve in the chow hall?"

Ernie was referring to creamed beef on toast, which GIs charmingly called shit on a shingle.

"No," I replied. "The original meaning—a call for assistance."

"So somebody's in there, trying to communicate with the outside world."

"Maybe they heard our voices."

"Why don't they just shout?"

"Probably somebody's watching and if they start shouting, they'll be punished."

"How?"

"How should I know? We need to get inside, see who it is, and find out what kind of help they need."

"That's us," Ernie said. "Full-service helpers." He pulled out the burglary tools he usually carried in his jacket pocket.

Kneeling, he studied the lock, then started poking it with a metal probe.

Inside, we descended cement steps into a dark chamber. We didn't want to turn on a light or use a flashlight, not yet; not until we understood the layout. I didn't want to alert anyone who might be waiting for us, so I felt my way forward, rubbing my palms along the cement wall, as quietly as I could. Finally, we reached a short flight of stairs that led up to a closed door haloed by light seeping around the edges. It reeked of burning oil and the sliced flesh of fish.

"The kitchen," Ernie whispered.

I was wondering what to do next when, off to our left, something hissed. At first I thought it was a snake, but then it hissed again, and I realized the voice was human and was making a *pssst* sound.

Ernie and I walked toward it.

High up on the far wall, just above ground level, moonlight glimmered through a small window, illuminating an enclosure with floor-to-ceiling metal stanchions that were attached to a thick mesh of welded chicken wire. Clutched fingers protruded through octagons.

"Had any *strange* lately?" a soft voice hissed.

A round face loomed out of the darkness. The shades, the cigarette holder, the slicked-back hair, the wrinkled khaki uniform.

"What the fuck are *you* doing here?" Ernie asked.

"I was about to ask you the same thing."

"That *nakji* guy," I said. "He locked you up?"

"His name's Shin," Strange replied. "Likes to be called Shin Sonseing-nim. Teacher Shin. I just call him Shin, without the honorifics, because he's an asshole."

"Locking you up sounds like a pretty good move to me," Ernie replied.

Strange rattled the fencing lightly. "I'm tired of the Count of Monte Cristo routine. Would you guys just get me the hell out of here?"

"You got a key?"

"They forgot to leave it with me."

Ernie studied the chainlink door, which was also locked. I decided to switch on the flashlight. Strange averted his eyes. Behind him, rows of tin cans lined wooden shelves, most of them sporting drawings of various types of sea life. So we were in the pantry. Upstairs, doors opened and slammed.

"No time for me to pick this damn thing," Ernie said. He looked up, studying the setup. "A row of bolts is holding the chicken wire in." He yanked on the wire. It didn't give. "Maybe with enough pressure."

More doors slammed upstairs. Words spoken rapidly in Korean were exchanged. The boys who'd been chasing us would have made their way past the charcoal briquettes now. I imagined they'd run up to the main drag, hadn't found us, then returned to the *nakji* place. Maybe to check in with their boss, maybe to keep searching for us.

Ernie got a better grip on the chicken wire and pulled down firmly, leaning his weight into it. "Come on," he said. "Help me with this."

Both Strange and I grabbed ahold of the wire above our heads, pulled down, and leaned backward to apply even more pressure. The overhead bolts didn't budge.

"We have to put our full body weight into it. Coordinated this time. On three, we all pull down. Ready? One, two, *three!*"

We pulled again and again. Finally, the bolts groaned, and on the fourth pull, wood started to crack and splinter.

Footsteps clomped downstairs.

"*Again!*" Ernie shouted, and this time the bolts gave way with one *pop* after another, raining down on us, and then the entire wall of chicken wire broke free and clattered to the ground. Without further orders, Ernie ran toward the exit. I helped Strange out and shoved him in front of me in the same direction. I dragged as much of the curled chicken wire across the floor as I could to form a barrier behind us.

Somebody shouted something in Korean, but by then we were already out the back door. Outside at the end of the alleyway, we paused to see if anyone was lying in wait for us.

"The road's empty," Ernie said after reconnoitering. He

pointed toward streetlamps and a row of glimmering neon. "The main drag is about fifty yards ahead. I say we make a run for it."

"Suits me," Strange said.

"You can handle it?" I asked him. He wasn't in the best shape in the world.

"I can handle it. And if those guys get anywhere near me, I'll sock 'em in the jaw."

"Should've tried that *before* they tossed you in with the canned mackerel," Ernie said.

Before they could start bickering, I said, "Come on," and led the way out toward the main road.

They caught up with us before we reached it.

Ernie didn't hesitate. He kicked and punched, and even though they had their clubs and knives, he took two of them down. Strange was being hit pretty hard, and one of the thugs backed him against a brick wall and started wailing away with a vengeance. He was about to crumble to the ground when I overcame one of the guys and managed to take his cudgel from him, then used it to chase him away. I whacked the guy attacking Strange right in the back of the head. He collapsed into a heap. Then I sat Strange up and slapped his face until his eyelids fluttered open.

"You okay?"

He groaned, and spittle tumbled out of his mouth. I bent

down, lifted him in the fireman's carry and started toward the light. Ernie followed, guarding our rear.

"Any more of them?" I asked.

"I think they've given up for now."

We reached the main drag. Open-mouthed Koreans stared at us as I staggered forward beneath Strange's considerable girth. Ernie led the way, and about a half-mile later, we found the jeep. Without worrying about whether or not he'd break any bones, I tossed Strange onto the back seat. He landed like a sack of spring cucumbers.

Ernie climbed behind the steering wheel, but before he started the engine, he glanced back at the almost-comatose Strange, then at me. "He fought," he said.

I nodded.

"And he came up with a plan to help save himself."

"Yeah. Morse code," I agreed.

Ernie nodded and started the engine.

I think that was the first time Agent Ernie Bascom had ever expressed anything resembling respect for the man called Strange.

-4-

At the emergency room entrance of the 121st Evacuation Hospital, we started to hoist Strange out of the back seat when, with renewed strength, he pulled away from us.

"Wait," he said. "Before we go in, you have to do something for me."

"What now?" Ernie asked.

Strange reached inside his shirt and pulled out a sheaf of paperwork. "Here. Give this to Orting. He'll know what to do with it." He twisted the document so the red light from the ER delivery ramp illuminated the cover sheet. It was light blue, with TOP SECRET blazoned atop.

"What the *hell* did you do?" Ernie asked. "You can't take this out of the head shed. What are you, nuts?"

A couple of medics pushed through double doors and walked out onto the elevated walkway. Strange glanced at them frantically, his face covered with perspiration.

"No time to explain now. Give this to Orting; he'll know what to do."

"Why should we?"

"Major Cranston will conduct a full classified-documents inventory tomorrow. He has to, by regulation."

"Because you disappeared for a day?"

Strange nodded. "Yes. You have to give this to Orting—tonight."

Ernie and I looked at each other. Messing with a misappropriated top-secret document wasn't something anybody with a brain would do lightly. But I hesitated before saying no. Maybe it was because of all the primo information Strange had provided to us in what must've been at least a dozen investigations that would've stalled for good otherwise. Or maybe it was because I didn't want to see 8th Army brass bring the hammer down yet again on an enlisted man. Whatever the reason, I grabbed the document from Strange, slid it under my shirt, and said, "Where can we find Orting?"

He told me.

"And who were those guys who attacked us, and why did this guy Shin lock you up?" I asked. "What's this all about?"

Before he could answer, one of the medics called out, "Hey, you going to bring that guy in, or what?"

"How about a gurney, for Christ's sake?" Ernie replied. "He can hardly walk."

We helped him up the stairs, and, as we did so, I told Strange to explain to me what the hell was going on.

"No time now," he said.

The medics brought out a gurney, sat him atop it, and told him to lie down. Then they rolled him into the building and the big double doors swung shut behind them.

Ernie parked the jeep in front of a two-story brick building with a sign emblazoned with a red and white cloverleaf symbol and below that, in large letters: HEADQUARTERS COMPANY, 8TH UNITED STATES ARMY. He turned off the ignition and held out his hand, expecting me to slap the document into it.

"No," I said. "I'll take it in."

"Forget it," Ernie replied. "You look too much like a cop."

Off-duty GIs are a suspicious lot. They imagine that truckloads of CID agents and even FBI investigators flown in from Washington, DC, are conducting clandestine surveillance, ready to bust them for something as small as smoking marijuana. The truth is that nobody really gives a damn. Why bother? What with a quarterly inspection of the barracks by a squad of MPs accompanied by drug-sniffing dogs, not to mention the semiannual urinalysis, GIs who smoke reefer will turn up soon enough. And a positive urine test is enough to get a guy kicked out of the army, as is a couple of joints found stuffed in a bagful of dirty laundry. I suppose it's human nature to think of oneself as important, so they treat the world as if it revolves around their petty GI problems. When strangers like us waltz into their midst, the young soldiers immediately begin to conjure elaborate fantasies of what they're up to.

Ernie fit in better with these paranoid soldiers. He'd served two tours in Vietnam, the first year hiding in his bunker and smoking high-potency hashish sold by snot-nosed boys outside the wire. The second year, according to Ernie, all the hash, even the marijuana, was gone, replaced conveniently enough by vials of pure China White. He'd become an addict, and when that tour was up, despite the war raging all around him, he didn't want to leave Vietnam.

As he told me more than once, "There'll never be another sweet one like that."

But leave Vietnam he did. And once he arrived here in Frozen Chosun, Ernie kicked the habit. He had no choice. In Korea, trafficking in heroin was punishable by death. And more than one wise-guy smuggler had been caught, tried, and hanged by the neck till dead. The word got out. Sell your poison someplace else, not in the Republic of Korea.

Luckily, another world-famous inebriate was readily available: alcohol. Ernie consumed it with abandon. Duty free, shipped to the brave soldiers abroad at taxpayer expense, its liberal employment fully approved by the honchos of the 8th United States Army.

Maybe it was his life experience, but somehow Ernie had a way with GIs. They saw him as another pothead, another user, another miscreant like them. Whether he was in a barroom, a pool hall, a brothel, or an after-duty barracks building, he blended in quickly and was readily accepted.

I handed him the top-secret document.

Ten minutes later, he came back and slid behind the steering wheel. "Found him. He told me he'd take care of it."

So Specialist Orting would slip the document Strange had stolen back into the classified documents cage, and even with Major Cranston conducting a full inventory tomorrow, no one would be the wiser. Or at least that was the plan.

Of course, the bigger questions were why Strange had taken the document in the first place and why those thugs had locked him up. What had they planned to do with him?

We'd found Strange and returned him to safety, which was what we'd set out to do, and even saved him and his cohorts from serious consequences. The next move was up to him.

Ernie started the engine. "Did you read the document?"

"No way. The less I know, the better." I turned to study him. "How about you? Did you read it?"

"Me? You think I'm stupid?"

I didn't answer.

Just glancing at a top-secret document without proper authorization or a need-to-know was a court-martial offense.

Ernie turned the jeep around, and as we made our way

through the quiet streets of Yongsan Compound, he said, "Hey, I'm an investigator. I had to look."

I didn't say anything.

"Do you want to know what it's about?"

"No," I answered.

"Okay." We passed the post bowling alley and kept rolling. "It's about Focus Lens," he said.

I groaned.

Focus Lens was the name of the joint ROK/US military exercise conducted every year by the Republic of Korea and the US as practice for our air, naval, and land forces to defend the country from another invasion from North Korea.

"Why'd you tell me that?" I asked.

"So you'll be in as much shit as I am if we're caught."

"Who's going to catch us? All we did was pick up a hurt GI, take him to the One-Two-One, and deliver a document for him."

"A *stolen* document."

"Let's not say *stolen*."

"And who knows who he shared it with."

"Not our business," I said.

"Bull," Ernie replied. "You know we should turn him in."

I did know, but said nothing.

"And what's Strange doing," Ernie continued, "taking out a top-secret document concerning an exercise that's scheduled to begin any day now?"

Focus Lens was always conducted in the early spring, but the exact kickoff date was classified.

Ernie turned to me. "Why'd he do that? And who the hell were those guys knocking him upside the head like that, keeping him as a prisoner?"

"Beats me."

"I still say we should report him."

I thought about it. To make sure that we weren't accused of abetting the misappropriation of a classified document, reporting everything that happened tonight to our boss, the 8th Army Provost Marshal, would've been the wise choice. CYA, as they say in the army: Cover Your Assets. But we'd already turned the document over to Orting. Still, we could claim we'd had a dumb attack, realized now the error of our ways, and probably get off with no more than a butt chewing. The longer we let this go on, the more trouble we were liable to be in. My hesitation stemmed from the fact that Strange had stuck his neck out for us too many times, providing classified information that, had it been traced back to him, could've landed him behind bars in the military stockade.

"I don't want to turn him in just yet," I said. "Let's see what he has to say. Maybe there's a good explanation."

Ernie grunted. "*That's* something I want to hear."

The next morning, Ernie and I made a couple of black-market arrests. Part of the reason we kept busy, I suppose, was to keep our minds off the misappropriated document and whether or not Strange would cause us any serious grief over it. By mid-afternoon, when we returned to the CID office, we figured Staff Sergeant Riley would be pleased at the improvement in our black-market stats. Instead, he stood behind his desk with his hands on his narrow hips, mouth twisted in annoyance.

"What?" Ernie asked. "Two arrests. You're not happy with that?"

"*Two* arrests?" Riley replied. "You're behind this month by about two *dozen.*"

Ernie shrugged and started toward the coffee urn in back.

"Hold it right there, soldier."

"What? A man doesn't have a right to a little hot coffee after a hard day's work?"

"The colonel wants to talk to you." Riley glanced at me. "Both of you. Right now."

I'd just reached out to hang my coat on the rack. I held it for a moment, frozen in fear. Had they already discovered the theft of the document? Had Strange told them of our involvement? As calmly as I could, I turned and asked, "What's this about?"

"Get down there like I told you and you'll find out."

"You're a big help, you are," Ernie said.

Riley plopped down in his chair. "Get me some more black-market arrests and maybe you'd receive a little more respect around here."

"Instead of being treated like dog shit."

Riley waved his pencil in the air. "I just wipe it off my shoe. Get down there and talk to the man. *Now*."

On the way out the door, Miss Kim flashed me a sympathetic smile.

At the end of the hallway, I paused for a moment and took a deep breath, composing myself. We entered the office of the 8th United States Army Provost Marshal, Colonel Walter P. Brace. He sat with pen in hand, diligently studying a stack of paperwork. Behind him, arrayed in their resplendent glory, were the flags of the United States, the United Nations command, and the Republic of Korea. We stood there in silence for a moment—I was trying to keep my breathing even—and when he put down his pen and looked up at us, Ernie and I both saluted. In response, Colonel Brace gave us a half-hearted wave and told us to sit. We sank into plush leather chairs.

Normally, when we received an ass-chewing, he kept us standing in front of his desk at the position of attention. Today, he seemed relaxed, almost friendly. As he relit his pipe and blew out a few puffs of smoke, I prepared myself for the worst. When he treated us like real human beings, like people worthy of civility, we were in for a ball-buster.

Ernie sensed it too. He kept his spine straight, not allowing himself to relax into the comfortable chair.

Once his pipe was finally drawing properly, Colonel Brace

set it in a large amber ashtray, folded his hands in front of his chest, and smiled.

"Good work on the black-market detail this morning," he said.

Ernie and I both fidgeted. *Here it comes*, I thought.

"However," he said, frowning, "your friend seems to be up to her usual shenanigans."

"What friend?" Ernie asked.

"Katie Byrd Worthington."

Inwardly, I breathed a deep sigh of relief. Katie Byrd Worthington was a reporter for a tabloid newspaper, the *Overseas Observer*. Notorious in the halls of 8th Army headquarters; she'd caused innumerable bouts of heartburn amongst the local brass, primarily for committing the unforgivable sin of publishing the truth. I had no interest in getting involved with her, but I was glad this wasn't about Strange.

"Katie Byrd is not our friend," Ernie protested.

Colonel Brace flashed a chilly smile. "She seems to think she is." He reached beneath a stack of paperwork and slid a report to the center of his desk. It was thin, only one or two sheets of paper, with a FOR OFFICIAL USE ONLY cover sheet. He lifted the top sheet and began to sum up the report.

"Last night in Seoul," he said, "in the Seongbuk-dong district, a certain Ms. Katie Byrd Worthington was arrested by the Korean National Police for creating a disturbance."

Ernie shook his head. "That sounds like her."

"It happened at the Samcheonggak resort area in a facility described as a 'traditional Korean entertainment venue.' Whatever that is."

I knew what it was. A *kisaeng* house. *Kisaeng* were elegant, well-educated women, who often served as entertainers at the royal court in ancient times. Similar to Japanese geisha.

"What exactly happened, sir?" I asked.

He looked back down at the report. "She interrupted a private dinner party and started snapping photographs. When one of the participants tried to stop her, she wrestled with him, knocking over a valuable celadon vase, and eventually kicked him in the groin area."

"That's definitely Katie," Ernie said.

"Anyone seriously hurt?" I asked.

"No. Just a few cuts and bruises." He continued to peruse the sheet. "Her camera was confiscated, along with the film, and she's currently being held at the KNP headquarters in Seoul."

"She's a civilian," Ernie said. "What's this got to do with us?"

"She mentioned your names to the KNPs."

"Us?"

"Yes. She told the KNPs you would vouch for her. Maybe accept responsibility for her so she could be released."

"Fat chance."

Whenever possible, the Korean National Police tried to avoid dealing with foreigners. Especially Americans. The authoritarian Park Chung-hee regime received millions of dollars from the US government in economic and military aid. The money helped solidify their hold on power. So an embarrassing incident with an American, especially one that might involve that American's congressional representative, was an irritant the Park government wouldn't be pleased about, and the lowest person on the totem pole, usually the local KNP commander, would be blamed. So if a face-saving way could be found to drop charges or otherwise smooth over the incident, the KNPs would find it.

Amused, Colonel Brace glanced back and forth at us. "I want you two to get over to the KNP headquarters. Now. Talk to her, get her to open up, even help spring her from jail if you have to. We want to know what in the hell she's up to."

"We" being the 8th Army honchos.

"She's trouble," Ernie replied.

"Don't I know it," Colonel Brace said. "We're hoping to avoid any more of those embarrassing articles in the *Overseas Observer.*"

Katie Byrd Worthington had previously exposed 8th Army personnel involvement in bank robbery and even human trafficking, running devastating headlines in the tabloid rag she worked for. The Department of Defense had tried more than once to shut down the *Overseas Observer*, but federal courts in the States had forced them to keep their hands off, even going so far as to order the US military to allow the *Oversexed*

Observer, as GIs called it, to be sold on the shelves of the Post Exchange. Published every Sunday, it sometimes competed in circulation with the DOD-authorized daily newspaper, the *Stars & Stripes*. Particularly when it blared out salacious headlines, always popular with GIs who hated the "Green Machine."

"So who did she kick?" Ernie asked.

Colonel Brace lifted his pipe, grabbed a cleaner, and started fiddling with it. "That's immaterial," he replied.

Once again, Ernie and I glanced at each other.

"Were Eighth Army personnel involved?" Ernie asked.

Exasperated, Colonel Brace set down his pipe. "*No.* Eighth Army personnel weren't involved in anything untoward."

It was a dodge. He'd denied only the "untoward" part, not the fact that they were involved in this in some way.

"So it's up to us to make sure that Katie Byrd kills the story."

Colonel Brace stared at Ernie steadily. "That would be nice, since no Eighth Army personnel were involved."

He'd pivoted to a flat-out denial. I could've pushed the point with him, but I knew better than to argue that the colonel had just contradicted himself. In the army, whether you're right or wrong is never based on logic. It's based only on one thing: rank. Colonel Brace outranked us, so he was right and we were wrong.

Without further explanation, we were dismissed. Ernie and I stood, saluted, and left his office.

As we walked down the hallway, Ernie whispered out of the side of his mouth, "He didn't say anything about Strange or the classified document."

"So far," I said.

"Yeah," Ernie replied. "Like the man said when he fell out a window of the Empire State Building and was halfway down, 'So far, so good.'"

The Korean National Police headquarters was located in the teeming downtown area of Seoul, two blocks from city hall, on the edge of a traffic circle that would've inspired Dante to add an extra layer to hell. Ernie cursed and honked as he bulled the little jeep through the swarm of trucks and military vehicles and kimchi cabs. "Doesn't anybody ever stay in their lane?" he asked.

"The white lines on the ground," I replied, "are merely aspirational."

"What?"

"Voluntary," I said.

Ernie twisted the steering wheel, barely avoiding a three-wheeled flatbed truck laden with an iridescent mountain of green Napa cabbage.

"Somebody ought to volunteer these drivers for the nut-house," Ernie said.

Finally, we made it into the small parking lot in front of the KNP headquarters. A khaki-clad officer blew his whistle and waved us forward. Ernie swerved the jeep beneath a cement overhang in front of the main entranceway.

The officer leaned into the side window. "No can do," he said in broken English. "Park car, no can do."

The lot behind us was completely full.

"This isn't a car," Ernie told the officer. "It's a jeep."

The officer gawked at us, not understanding. Ernie pulled the jeep over to the curb, switched off the ignition, and looped a thick chain welded to the metal floorboard through the steering wheel. Once the chain held firm, he snapped a padlock between opposing links. We both climbed out of the jeep.

The officer tweeted his whistle and glared at us but did nothing as we pushed our way through the revolving glass door. Inside, the tiled foyer reeked of kimchi and cheap tobacco smoke. We paused at the reception desk and told the uniformed female officer who we wanted to talk to.

We could've asked directly to see the American woman being held, Katie Byrd Worthington, but I'd decided that it would be best to check in with the man we'd worked with on at least half a dozen cases so far: Gil Kwon-up, Chief Homicide Inspector for the Korean National Police. The man GIs in law enforcement called "Mr. Kill." For the last year and a half, he'd acted in many ways as our mentor, guiding us through the catacomb-like passageways of Korean law enforcement. Not to mention advising us on the best ways to catch a crook. He'd been doing this job since the end of the Korean War, just slightly over twenty years, and he'd managed to work his way up from a cop on the beat to top detective in the country.

The receptionist picked up a phone, spoke into it, and after she hung up, pointed to a varnished wooden bench on the far wall. We sat and Ernie leaned forward, perusing the police officials, some in uniforms, some in civilian suits, parading back and forth.

"Maybe we ought to leave her locked up," he said.

"That'll just make her angry, and next week's *Oversexed Observer* will probably feature us."

"What can she possibly say about me? I'm a saint."

"Yeah, the Bishop of Itaewon."

"Hey, I like that. I could walk around the barrooms and nightclubs waving one of those things. What do you call 'em?" He mimicked swinging a heavy object from the end of a chain. "You know, with incense."

"A censer," I said.

"Right. A censer. That oughta earn me a free drink or two."

"Probably just get you locked up with Katie Byrd."

A female officer strode toward us. She was trim and healthy-looking, and her cotton blouse and pressed blue skirt fit her like she'd been born in them. When she nodded, the upturned brim of her brass pillbox cap glinted under the overhead lights.

This was Officer Oh, personal assistant to Mr. Kill.

Her posture was so upright, she almost leaned backward.

"Good morning, Agent Sueño, Agent Bascom," she said, nodding to each of us. "You want to see Mrs. Worthington?"

She's not a "Mrs.," I thought, but rather than correct her, I said, "Yes. How'd you know that?"

"Arresting officer, he report to us that she ask for you. Inspector Gil, he expect you soon."

"But she's a civilian," Ernie said. "Why would Inspector Kill expect us to come here whether she asked for us or not?"

"Ah, she is a newspaper reporter. Very important."

In America, I thought. *Not so much here in Korea.*

"This way," she said and turned on her heels.

Ernie and I followed her past the elevators, down a short hallway, and then she turned again and we descended one, two, three flight of stairs. She pushed through a heavy door and held it for us until we caught up. Now the stairway was single-file, and dim bulbs encased in metal cages fought a losing battle against the gloom. Even the air was colder.

As we twisted downward, Ernie said, "Spooky."

Finally, after descending four more levels, Officer Oh stopped and pushed through another heavy door. Painted on it in white lettering was a single Chinese character: *yo*, meaning woman.

"There," she said, pointing toward the right. "Second door."

We hurried over to an iron grating, where inside something screeched and then a woman screamed.

-5-

"About time you got me out of that damn cell," Katie Byrd said. "It's like the Middle-freaking-Ages around here." She was wearing a dark-blue jumpsuit that looked like a gunney sack stuffed with knives on her wiry body.

"I wouldn't use the past tense," I told her. "We haven't sprung you yet."

We sat at a wooden table in a cramped room meant for visitors. There were no amenities—no vending machines, no coffee maker, only four or five scratched wooden tables and a smattering of three-legged stools. A chubby-faced male guard loomed at the doorway. Conveniently, the tiny refuge was placed near the *byonso*. A stench like a mile-wide sewer pinpointed the crapper as efficiently as a topographical map.

"Oh, come *on*, you guys. You're not gonna refuse to sign for me, are you?"

The KNPs had agreed to release Katie Byrd if a responsible

authority from US Forces Korea vouched for her future good conduct.

"What about your fancy *Overseas Observer* lawyer?" Ernie asked. "Why doesn't he get you out?"

"He will," she said. "But not for a couple days. He's in Hong Kong, for Christ's sake."

"So you don't need us," I said.

She grabbed my wrist. "Yes, I *do*. My cellmate is going to kill me if I don't get out of here soon."

"Why'd you scream when we reached your cell?" Ernie asked.

"That wasn't me. That was *her*. That crazy broad murdered her husband, and the way she was looking at me, I'm pretty sure she thought I was him."

It figured that the Korean authorities had tossed Katie Byrd into a cell with a dangerous inmate, probably to teach her a lesson. This government didn't like reporters, especially when they were running around free. The Korean press operated at the sufferance of the Park Chung-hee regime, and any deviation from government policy could not only get a newspaper shut down, but could also land the journalist—not to mention his editor and publisher—in a jail cell. But the Korean government had little control over the *Overseas Observer*, an independent American newspaper. Still, they didn't want to rescind their press credentials and kick them out of the country, because expelling her from the country would be a slap in the face to the so-called American way of life—the free press and all that. And if the media back in the States got ahold of the story, they could give South Korea a metaphorical black eye. But what the Korean government could do now, given Katie Byrd's indiscretion, was take advantage of the incident by charging her with assault and locking her up in jail with a madwoman.

"They're sending you a message," I told her.

"Don't I know it. And they're not using Western Union." She rubbed her face, as if she hadn't slept much.

"So if you don't want to wait for your fancy lawyer," Ernie said, "and you want us to spring you from here, there's a few things you have to promise."

She leaned her elbows on the table and locked eyes with him. "If it's sexual favors you want, you got it, Big Boy."

He crossed his arms. Katie Byrd Worthington was the only woman I'd ever known who could make Ernie Bascom squirm. She wasn't bad-looking, thin and spry, with a pug nose and blue eyes beneath a mop of short-cropped blonde hair, probably in her mid-thirties—almost a decade older than Ernie or me. She claimed to be from Fort Worth, Texas, but my guess was that she hadn't grown up in a city. I imagined a hardscrabble homestead, a farm or ranch outside of town with no running water and few modern amenities with a whole lot of chores to be done. We'd worked with her—or perhaps *struggled* with her, to be more precise—on a previous case, and that was the impression she gave. Self-assured, determined, and able to take on the challenges of life. But even for Katie Byrd Worthington, being stuck in a dungeon beneath the streets of Seoul with a convicted murderer for company appeared to be more than she had bargained for.

Finally, since the first time we'd known her, Ernie and I were holding all the cards.

"No story," Ernie said, waggling his finger at her, "about whatever was going on at that fancy *kisaeng* house you were at."

"Samcheonggak," I said, to let her know we knew which *kisaeng* house she'd been at.

"No story? Are you guys nuts? Do you have any idea who was there that night and what they were doing?"

"No," Ernie said, "and we don't give a damn, either. Not our business."

"Well, it ought to be. *Chaebol*. Do you know what that means?"

Ernie didn't. She turned to me.

"It's like a conglomerate," I said. "A group of interconnected corporations."

"With excellent government connections, don't forget," she added. "They're conspiring to rip off the US taxpayer, in addition to abusing women."

"Well, everybody abuses women," Ernie said.

"Don't I know it," she said, rubbing her bare arms. "But if they were just boffing a few *kisaeng* girls, I wouldn't have much of a story."

"So what are they doing?" I asked.

She leaned even closer to me. I smelled something on her breath—gruel, maybe, and fermented turnips.

"The Korean elites are wining and dining these guys because they want US Defense Department contracts. Also, they're setting up relations with the high-tech military contractors and, through them, looking into civilian applications for things like television and other electronics."

"So?" Ernie said. "Isn't that what they're supposed to do? They're in business, aren't they?"

"Yeah, but there are payoffs. First, they set the Eighth Army honchos up with a girl, and later there are cash payouts. Bags of American dollars. Sometimes Japanese yen. Going directly to high-ranking American officers."

"Bull," Ernie said. "How do you know this?"

Katie crossed her arms. "That's my business. And I've got the goods to prove it."

I thought about it. "Listen, Katie, what Eighth Army is most worried about is what's going to appear in this Sunday's edition of the *Overseas Observer*. They want no story. No photographs. Nothing." I paused; she was listening to me intently. "What you do with the rest of your information, if it appears in some outside international news organization, that's up to you. As long as no compromising photos of American military officers ever see the light of day."

"Why are they so worried about pictures?"

Ernie spoke up. "Nobody ever reads the stories in the *Oversexed Observer*. They just skim the headlines and look at the photos. Especially of the girls in bikinis."

The *Observer* always included at least two or three talent agency photos of scantily clad models frolicking on beaches. That, along with the salacious headlines and the stateside advertisements for things like sports cars and booze and hair cream, was what the average GI zeroed in on. There was even a weekly feature with a mail-order coupon that a lonely GI could cut out and send in along with a money order to have an engagement ring mailed directly to his girl back home.

"I know nobody reads the stories," Katie Byrd said, "except for the brass. And I love aggravating them. But whether anybody reads it or not, I have to fill up my column inches."

"Fill it up with something other than this *chaebol* story," I said, seeing that she was weakening. "And no photos that make Eighth Army look ridiculous."

"It *is* ridiculous." She suddenly seemed sad. "The KNPs confiscated the only roll of film I had in my camera. You must know that. I won't be able to run any of the photos. So what are you worried about?"

"The KNPs still have it?" I asked.

"Yeah. Unless they burned it already."

"We'll check with them," I said.

"But if we make a deal, I'm not going to let this censorship last forever. Any other photos I have, past or future—no restrictions on them."

"That sounds fine," I said. After all, Colonel Brace had only expressed worry about the photos she'd taken after barging into the *kisaeng* party. "And no written story about the *chaebol*."

She glanced around the bare room, rubbing her arms compulsively.

"All right," she said. "*This* story doesn't appear in the *Overseas Observer*. But, again, if I find a new story in the future, that's fair game."

"Okay," I said.

"But you have to get me out *now*. Right now. I'm not going back into that cell with that lunatic."

"She'll miss you," Ernie said.

"Cry me a river," Katie Byrd responded.

The tow truck was just backing up to the front of the jeep.

Ernie pushed through the revolving door and sprinted toward the back of the truck, then stood between it and his jeep.

"*Halt!*" he shouted. "Hold it right there."

Slowly, the tow truck kept backing up. I ran around the front of the truck and confronted the driver through the open window. "*Jeongji!*" I shouted. Halt. Startled, he finally stepped on the brakes.

The armed guard who had ordered us not to park there in the first place approached, this time with backup—two more armed guards. They were screaming at me in Korean, speaking so fast that I couldn't make out most of it, but their meaning was clear. We'd parked in a restricted area, and our jeep had to be confiscated. Ernie cursed and made rude hand gestures but didn't budge from his strategic spot between jeep and tow truck.

All of Katie Byrd's possessions, save the film, had been returned, so now she was in full regalia: sneakers, khaki pants, matching jungle jacket with multiple pockets, and an Australian bush hat pinned atop her bobbed hair. She pulled out her trusty Nikon camera from the canvas camera bag hanging at her side and began snapping photos, crouching and prowling around us like a wildlife photographer in the Serengeti.

More guards were arriving on scene, curious at first, but once they realized what was going on, their expressions changed from surprise to anger. Nobody liked a couple of arrogant foreigners thinking that the rules didn't apply to them. From some of the comments they made, often starting with *uri nara,* "our country," I gleaned that they felt that the refusal by Ernie and me to submit to KNP authority was not only a breach of the law but also an insult to Korea and, by proxy, Koreans everywhere.

Generally, the citizens of South Korea supported the presence of the fifty thousand-plus American military personnel in their country. They understood that America's might was a profound deterrent from further aggression by the Communist regime up north. But when that acceptance was pierced by rude American behavior, the nationalist tendencies of a proud five-thousand-year-old culture could sometimes boil over.

Ernie was still swearing and raising his fist and shouting that no one was going to touch his jeep. I wished profoundly that he'd shut the hell up. Some of the guards started to move toward him.

Suddenly, as if a switch had been flipped, everyone quieted down. I turned in the direction everyone else was gazing. Mr. Gil Kwon-up strode through the front door. His short black hair, flecked with gray at the sides, was combed straight back, and he wore a suit and an overcoat that even someone who shopped in the PX, like me, could tell had been imported from more than a few countries away. His face was grim as he approached the ranking guard. The man bowed and saluted, then explained in rapid Korean what had happened, occasionally pointing at Ernie and me. Inspector Gil listened gravely. Finally, after the guard was finished, almost exhausted because of the long speech, Inspector Gil turned to me.

He motioned for me to approach. As I did, the khaki-clad guard bowed and backed away. I stood in the same spot where the guard had just been and bowed deeply to the illustrious detective.

I knew all this was about saving face, not allowing foreigners to walk all over the Korean people as had happened so often since the turn of the century. First when the Japanese had invaded in 1910, deposed the royal family, and even kidnapped the crown prince and forced him to live in Japan. And at the end of World War II, despite being liberated from Japan, the Korean people had to suffer the ignominy of having American soldiers occupy the south of their country while the Soviet Army occupied the north. Then the Korean War had exploded, with fighters from all over the world tromping up and down the peninsula, defiling ancient temples, raping Korean women, slaughtering Korean men by the hundreds of thousands. And finally, after the war, the shame of poverty, with Korea seen as an economic basket case comparable with the poorest countries in the world.

Inspector Gil frowned at me disapprovingly. Ernie fidgeted behind me, still protecting the front bumper of his beloved army-issue jeep. He loved that jeep, mainly because every month he paid a quart of Johnny Walker Black to the head dispatcher at the 8th Army motor pool to not only reserve the jeep for him exclusively, but also make sure the vehicle was well-maintained, topped off with fuel, and always equipped with tires that had plenty of tread. Ernie had gone so far as to pay out of his own pocket for tuck-and-roll vinyl upholstery to be installed in the back seat, replacing the rough army-issue canvas. And no one should mess with his laughing devil gear-shift knob, his pride and joy. I knew Ernie would put up a fight for the honor of his jeep.

Gruffly, Inspector Gil asked, "*Weigurei no nun?*" What is it with you?

It was spoken with a disrespectful verb ending, as if from a learned superior to an uneducated lout whom he found to be beneath contempt.

Ernie didn't like these displays. He thought they were demeaning to Americans and American culture. And maybe they were. But I knew it was an act, and I was flattered that Gil Kwon-up trusted me enough to have me help resolve a dispute that might otherwise prove to be damaging to US relations with the Korean police and maybe even explode into something dangerous. We'd worked together many times. I liked to think that we understood each other. Mr. Kill was a highly educated man. He'd not only earned a university degree here in Korea, but as a child he'd been tutored in the Four Books and the Five Classics, the canon of ancient Confucian education of the Far East. In addition, years ago, he'd been selected to attend an Ivy League university in the States and study as a fellow for two years in conjunction with a Department of Defense program designed to shore up law enforcement support for anti-Communist operations. An important contribution to the Free World's conduct of the Cold War.

So when he asked me this blunt question in such a

demeaning manner, I didn't flinch. In a voice loud enough for all the guards to hear, I spoke in Korean, explaining that when we arrived there were no parking spaces in the lot and we were under a time constraint since the woman we were here to retrieve was in danger for her life if we didn't find her right away. Kill didn't respond. I went on. "I apologize to this man"—I gestured with my open hand toward the main guard—"and to all of the hard-working policemen here for the trouble I've caused. I apologize to the good inspector and to the Korean National Police in general."

I bowed again.

A murmur of approval went through the crowd. Inspector Gil barked an order. "Everyone back to work."

The men dispersed.

The tow-truck driver, who'd emerged from his truck and had been listening, climbed back into the cab, started the engine, and drove off.

Ernie walked over to me. "What the hell did you say?"

"I told them that we were on official Eighth Army business, and we Americans were paying most of their country's defense bills and putting ourselves on the line to protect them from the Commies, and that they had no business bothering us in any way."

"Good. That shut 'em the hell up."

Satisfied, he and Katie climbed into the jeep. Him behind the steering wheel, her sitting on the tuck-and-roll in back.

I approached Inspector Gil. "Thank you," he said, "for your diplomacy."

"I try to give both sides what they want."

"Different languages help in that endeavor."

"Greatly," I said.

He reached into the pocket of his overcoat and pulled something out. A sheet of thick paper, rolled but not creased. He handed it to me. In the overhead light, I opened it and studied the contact sheet, a preliminary print of the snapshots from a roll of film. Each photo was small, no larger than a thumbprint, but clear enough for newspaper editors and other professionals to use and decide which shots were worthy of being enlarged to appear in a newspaper or a magazine.

I studied the photos, squinting to make out what I was seeing. A *kisaeng* party. Korean men in suits and American men in military uniforms seated around a low table laden with chopsticks and spoons and a multitude of delicacies in porcelain bowls. One, or in some cases two, beautiful young *kisaeng* were serving and entertaining each guest. Cups were lifted in toasts, soju and beer were poured. Halfway through the photos, the women were standing and appeared to be coaxing the men upright and encouraging them to dance. And then a few of the women had taken off various items of clothing, and one of the American men, with a barrel chest and pot belly, naked down to the waist, had joined them. He had grabbed chopsticks and was using them in obscene ways. Mercifully, the photos of the party ended there. There was only one more photo at the end: an angry Korean cop reaching out his hand to smother the camera lens.

"This woman," Mr. Kill said, nodding toward the jeep, "this Katie Byrd Worthington. She is very resourceful."

"Yes, sir. And a pain in the butt."

He nodded, a slight twinkle in his eyes. "I wish she were working for us."

"Good luck recruiting her." I glanced down at the contact sheet. "What about the film?"

"It is in a safe place."

"This man," I said, "the one who took his shirt off and was acting so foolishly, you know who he is, don't you?"

"Oh, yes. We are well aware of who he is."

We both were. In Korean and US military circles, he was famous. One of the most powerful men in the country. Brigadier General Hubert N. Frankenton, Chief of Staff of the 8th United States Army.

"Wouldn't you rather turn the film over to General Frankenton, so he can destroy it and rest easy knowing it won't be used against him?"

"Personally, yes. I would rather do that. But my superiors are . . . what's the word? Machiavellian. They want to keep the film."

"As leverage in case they need it someday."

Mr. Kill shrugged and spread the fingers of his right hand. "Such is the way of the world."

"But I can assure Eighth Army that it won't be published?"

"We have no such plans." He hesitated, then added, "Currently."

I knew that was the best guarantee I was likely to receive. If the 8th Army honchos didn't want other people to have such embarrassing information on them, maybe they should stop attending *kisaeng* parties. Or at least stop making fools of themselves at them.

I thanked Inspector Kill, saluted him, and returned to the jeep.

"What did *he* want?" Katie asked, leaning forward from the back seat.

"He gave me this," I told her, tossing the contact sheet into the back seat.

"These are *my* photos," she said.

"They were. You committed a crime, the Korean Police confiscated your film, and now those shots belong to them."

"That's unconstitutional," she said.

"Maybe under our constitution," I told her, "but not theirs."

She studied the photos. "Not bad, considering the angle I had to shoot from."

"Which was?" Ernie asked.

"Through a partially open heating duct with a conveniently small hole twisted out of the grating."

"A hole created by you?"

"Would I do something like that?"

"*Yes*," Ernie said.

Ignoring Ernie's comment, she stretched as the little jeep swerved through traffic. "My joints are still out of whack from lying there for over an hour."

"You're a dedicated journalist, Katie," Ernie said.

"You better believe it." She leaned forward and, this time, ran her hand along the back of Ernie's seat, then caressed his shoulder. "Since you've got plenty of gas, could you do me one teeny, tiny favor?"

"*What?*" Ernie snapped.

"Well, you know I'm just a poor little country girl."

"Knock off the bullshit," Ernie warned.

"My mother, before she died, God rest her soul, gave me a necklace that was handed down to her from her mother and from her grandmother before that. She entrusted me with it."

"Yeah, yeah, yeah," Ernie said. "Get to the point."

"It's small, made of silver, and has a cross with a heart attached to it. Like, you know, the love of Jesus. When she gave it to me, she made me promise never to lose it."

"So you lost it."

"Hey, it wasn't my fault. Those damn Korean cops took it."

"They didn't return it to you?"

"No. They returned everything else I was wearing when they took me in, but the necklace must've fallen off during the roughhousing after somebody spotted me snapping the photos. I thought I could make a break for it through the garden surrounding the *kisaeng* house, but they grabbed me as I was crawling out of the heating duct."

"Tough break," Ernie said.

"So I was hoping that you two guys, what with your military jeep and your emergency Eighth Army dispatch and CID badges and all, could take me back there and help me look for it. My mother will never forgive me for losing it. Especially here in this heathen country."

"It's not a heathen country," I told her. "Buddhism's been here for at least as long as it's been in China. And that's a long time."

"I'm talking about Christianity."

"There are more Christians in Korea than anywhere else in Asia—except the Phillippines," I told her.

"Really? How many?"

"Millions," I said.

"Well, okay, maybe it's not so heathen."

"And where do you get off calling anybody 'heathen'?" Ernie asked. "You work for the *Oversexed Observer*, for Christ's sake."

"Don't swear."

"I'll swear if I goddamn want to."

"All right, children," I said. "Let's not bicker."

"So will you do it?" Katie Byrd asked. "Help me find my necklace?"

"What do we get out of it?" Ernie asked.

"Well, you already lost your chance for sexual favors." Katie seemed to think about it. "I'll tell you what. If we find the necklace, I'll treat you both to all the beer you can drink in the cocktail lounge of the Bando Hotel."

"Whoop-de-doo," Ernie said.

The Bando was the oldest Western-style hotel in Seoul, a thick-walled cement building constructed during the Japanese colonial period, sturdy enough to have withstood the bombardment of the Korean War. The cocktail lounge was shabby and old-fashioned and filled with ancient geezers who lived in the past. Not the kind of joint any self-respecting bar-hopper like Ernie Bascom would be found in trying to pick up a girl.

"I'll throw in peanuts," Katie said.

Ernie mulled over the offer. "The two food groups. Beer and peanuts."

"That's right," Katie said. "It'll restore your health."

"My health is just fine, thank you."

Actually, going to the scene of Katie Byrd Worthington's last-known affront to the dignity of the 8th United States Army wasn't a bad idea. Not only could we examine the site of the alleged incident, but it would also give us the chance to glean more information from Katie and perhaps other bystanders as to what had actually happened.

But mostly, I was tired of listening to them argue.

"Turn right up here," I told Ernie, pointing at the next large intersection. That was the road that led to Samcheonggak, the elite resort area where Katie had been arrested.

Katie clapped her hands in glee. "You won't regret it," she said.

"We'll see about that," Ernie replied.

-6-

We left the city and climbed toward a row of craggy peaks. Soon a two-story road led us through a thickening forest of pines. Finally, a handwritten placard directed us to the right. Two hundred yards in, a sign overhead read SAMCHEONGGAK, the Pavilion of the Three Purities. A brightly colored gate was guarded by two wooden poles with carved visages: on the left, the Great General of Heaven and, on the right, the Great General of the Underworld. Ten yards past these terrifying deities, a more practical obstacle blocked our way. A guard shack manned by two ROK Army soldiers. One of them, cradling an automatic rifle in the crook of his arm, stepped forward and waved us to a halt.

I spoke to him in Korean, explaining that we were from 8th Army and had to examine the site where General Frankenton, the Chief of Staff, had been assaulted. He studied our emergency dispatch, handed it back to us, and demanded to see our identification. As he studied our CID badges he called out the serial numbers, and the guard inside the shack appeared to be writing them down.

"Tough security up here," Ernie said.

"That's because the president and his cronies use this area as their personal playground," Katie said. "Their own cozy little resort. Hot and cold, running women and everything else their testosterone-shriveled little hearts could desire."

"How do I apply for membership?" Ernie asked.

After handing back our badges, the guard motioned toward Katie. She pulled out her passport and handed it to him. Again, he called out the serial number but before handing the passport back to Katie, he asked me in Korean, "Why is she with you?"

"She's the perpetrator," I told him. "We're taking her back to the scene of the crime to force her to confess."

This seemed to correspond with his Confucian sense of justice. Nine out of ten times in a Korean courtroom, an accused criminal not only admitted to his crimes but also asked for forgiveness from his victims and society in general. That way, healing could begin, allowing the judge to show mercy. But God help those accused of heinous acts who maintained their innocence. They would not only stand convicted of the offense but also of the larger crime of calling the prosecutors who accused them liars. Something that didn't go down well with judges, all of whom came from the most elite strata of Korean life.

The guard handed the passport back to Katie, stood back, and waved us on. As we left, his cohort on the phone kept talking, apparently reciting the data that had just been gathered.

Ernie shifted from first to second gear and said, "That was easy."

"Too easy," I responded.

"Yeah. They'll be on us soon enough."

Katie Byrd pounded her small fist against the back of my seat. "Let's just knock off the speculation and hurry."

Ernie shifted into third.

He drove us up a meandering single-lane pathway lined on either side with forest, manmade ponds, geese, lawns, flower gardens, and neatly tended shrubs. Finally, Katie pointed toward a horseshoe-shaped driveway. At the end, a tile-roofed building made of brightly painted carved wood sat by itself.

"This is it?" Ernie asked.

"This is it," Katie replied. "Romper Room for the boys with stars on their shoulders or a few hundred million *won* in the bank."

Ernie came to a stop and shut down the engine. "How'd you find it?" he asked. "And how'd you know they would be having a *kisaeng* party?"

"Sources," she replied and pushed her way out of the jeep. Without waiting for us, she trotted toward the rear of the building. By the time we managed to reach the backyard area, she had disappeared.

"What the . . . " Ernie said.

I pointed at a heating flue cover laying flat on the ground.

"Oh, for Christ's sake." Ernie lowered himself to the ground and stared into the flue. "She's in there," he said, rising to his feet and slapping grass off his pants. "Already on the far side climbing upward. All I could see were her sneakers."

"Let's look around," I said.

The front door was made of varnished oak and what appeared to be handcrafted brass plates. I tried the handle. Locked. We found a side door secured this time by a padlock on the outside that Ernie was able to pry open with one of the tools he kept handy for just such an eventuality. Inside, the building was dark and cool, and our feet clattered on immaculate wooden flooring.

"Shouldn't we take off our shoes?" I said.

"You worry too much, Sueño."

Ernie slid back one of the oil-papered latticework doors, revealing a narrow room filled with a low rectangular table lined with flat cushions for seating. At the far wall, a small closet, maybe filled with what I imagined would be serving implements. I peeked inside. Instead, it housed a sound system and microphones attached to long, coiled cords.

"Music, dancing, singing," I said. "And plenty of booze and snacks, all served by *kisaeng.*"

"A good enough combination," Ernie said, "to entice General Frankenton into making a fool of himself."

Metal rattled. From between the narrow slats of a heating vent, small fingers protruded.

"Katie," I said, squatting. "Is that you?"

"It ain't the Cookie Monster," she replied in a muffled voice.

"That's where you took the pictures from?"

"And twisted my spine like pulled taffy, thank you very much."

"Didn't they hear the camera clicking or whirring or whatever?"

"They were *drunk*," she shouted, tin rattling behind her as she moved away. "Plus, the whole room was filled with music and the girls' clapping and the men's awful singing."

Ernie knelt next to me. "Did you find the necklace?"

"Not yet."

Outside, an internal combustion engine roared toward us, accompanied by the sound of tires kicking up gravel. Ernie left to investigate.

I leaned closer to the vent. "Somebody's coming. Time for us to leave."

I joined Ernie at the front door.

He peeped through stained glass. "*Honbyong*," he said. Korean military police.

Without further discussion, we both returned to the side door and exited, locking it behind us. We found Katie at the back of the building, straightening her pants and shirt.

"You guys get out there," she told us. "Stall 'em. When I

hear the jeep's engine start, I'll run out and jump in the back seat."

Technically, we hadn't done anything wrong. We hadn't stolen or vandalized anything, but still, we had trespassed our way into a supposedly secure building patrolled by the Korean Army, and it was certain they'd be unhappy about that. Neither Ernie nor I wanted to be held for the rest of the day waiting for some hotshot ROK Army investigator to come and interrogate us. And Katie, as a reporter in a country that hated reporters, could be locked up again. On what charge? They didn't need a particular charge—any trumped-up reason would do.

Ernie and I walked out front, keeping our hands fully visible at our sides, and presented ourselves to the Korean MPs. There was a half dozen of them, three in each vehicle, and their ranking man had two silver starbursts on his cap, making him a lieutenant colonel. I bowed and said, "*Anyonghaseiyo?*"

He responded in English. "Why you here?" He pointed at the building.

"General Frankenton was here last week." It's always good to start a conversation with a suspicious military officer by mentioning someone of a higher rank. "Someone took photographs of the general. Not supposed to. We came to find out how."

My statement was an implicit criticism of him and the ROK Army security in this area. His face turned red. "Not supposed to," he said, sputtering. "You must check with us first. You understand? Us first."

I nodded. "I am sorry. Next time, we will check with you first." I bowed even deeper. Ernie mercifully kept his mouth shut.

We presented our badges; he made a show of jotting information in his notebook and brusquely handed them back to us. He said a few more words, which once again were just for show, and waggled his forefinger at us. The truth was that taking a couple of Americans into custody would be more trouble than he wanted. He'd have to report it up the chain of command and would then be questioned about why he was disrupting a delicate diplomatic dance between the two governments. He'd end up having to explain himself, in great detail, to his superiors. Better to huff and puff and let us go. Which he finally did, waving his arm dismissively as if he were sick of the entire situation.

Ernie and I hurried to the jeep. Ernie started the engine, shoved the gear shift into reverse, and backed up toward the side of the building. Katie Byrd appeared around the corner and jumped into the back seat.

As we sped away, the colonel glared at us, and then one of his men was shouting and pointing, apparently having realized that an unaccounted-for civilian had just joined us. The MPs ran back to their vehicles and the engines roared to life.

I turned around in my seat. "They're coming after us."

Ernie laughed and patted the flat metal dashboard. "They'll never catch this baby. I just paid for new spark plugs."

Always the reporter, Katie leaned forward and said, "You have to *pay* for the maintenance of an army vehicle?"

"He wants it done quickly," I told Katie.

"And I want it done right," Ernie added, "by the most experienced mechanic. A quart of Johnny Walker Black each month to the head dispatcher does the trick."

Katie laughed and sat back.

The *honbyong* behind us switched on their sirens.

Ernie stepped on the gas.

A half-mile down the road leaving Samcheonggak, we passed through a long tunnel, and when we emerged, they were still on our tail. For the next mile or so, Ernie let the little jeep loose, making us lean as he took the corners with just a bare hint of a skid. He gained some distance, but not enough for us to lose them. After another half-mile, the ancient defensive wall surrounding Gyeongbokgung Palace loomed on our right. Originally built in the fourteenth century by the rulers of the Chosun Dynasty, the palace had been burnt down periodically by foreign invaders—the Japanese and others—but had recently been renovated to its past glory. The dozens of edifices and gardens and shrines no longer housed a royal family, however. Their ancient legacy was reduced to a theme park for tourists, showcasing the traditional culture of Korea for the legions of natives and foreigners who had the few hundred *won* required to gain admittance.

Fortunately—or unfortunately, as I thought at the time—a metal gate had been opened to allow a garbage truck to exit the massive grounds of the palace. We'd just rounded a curve, so our pursuers weren't yet visible behind us. The garbage truck fully emerged, partially blocking the road. Ernie zipped around it, hung a hard right, and, taking the turn on two wheels, squeezed between the truck and the open gate onto the grounds of the palace.

After the jeep bounced back on all four tires, I shouted, "What in the *hell* are you doing?"

He ignored me and sped his way past the magnificent palaces and gurgling fountains and phalanxes of Asian tourists holding guidebooks and wearing cheap hats to block the sun. Ahead, a row of soldiers paraded across the well-swept grounds, all sporting knee-length tunics made of red silk, black horsehair hats, and holding pikes topped with wickedly curved metal points. Beyond them, a troop of a half-dozen mounted men, similarly attired, went through a routine of intricately syncopated maneuvers.

"Who are they?" Katie asked.

"The palace guard," I told her.

Ernie swerved around their formation and soon we approached the front gate. The pedestrian entrances next to the ticket booths were only wide enough for one person at a time and each exit was blocked by a revolving door made of iron bars.

"Trapped," Katie said.

"Not yet," Ernie replied. He backed up and made his way toward the stables where the king's cavalry was quartered. "Horseshit," Ernie said. "They must have to take it out every day, or the tourists would be forced to wear gas masks."

And he was right. There was a wooden gate there, large enough for a two-and-a-half-ton truck, but it was closed. He pulled up next to it, and I hopped out and slid back the iron rod holding it shut. When I pulled the gate open, Ernie drove the jeep through. I hollered at him to wait as I took the time to shove the gate shut. Then I jumped into the passenger seat.

"Always so fastidious, huh, Sueño?"

"Hey, we've caused them enough disruption."

Ernie seemed to remember something. He leaned his head back and said, "So, Katie, when exactly did you kick General Frankenton in the balls?"

"When he tried to grab me. I crawled back out of the vent, and all those Korean and American blowhards were screaming at me and waving to security to come and take me away. Frankie Baby got all grabby and tried to frisk me, pretending he was looking for a roll of film."

"But he wasn't?"

"Hell, no. First thing he does, he reaches for my bra. There's no way I could hide a roll of film in there. I ain't exactly Jayne Mansfield, if you haven't noticed."

Ernie barked a laugh and almost swerved off the road.

Two blocks ahead, Ernie stopped at a busy intersection. We had reached the outskirts of downtown Seoul, with all its swirling kimchi cabs and delivery vehicles and rapid-transit vehicles. No sign of the *honbyong*.

"They'll never find us now," Ernie said.

I didn't want to encourage the turbocharged antics that had almost gotten us killed more than once, but, silently, I had to admit that Agent Ernie Bascom was a whiz behind the wheel.

Katie started to clamber over me. "I'll get out here," she said.

"Hey," Ernie shouted. "What about my beer and peanuts?"

"We didn't find the necklace," she shouted, already trotting away, clutching her canvas camera bag to prevent it from bouncing. She started running, not bothering to look back.

Ernie turned to me. "I think we've been had."

I nodded. "I doubt there was ever a necklace."

We watched as she hailed a kimchi cab, leaned toward the passenger window, and spoke to the driver.

"So if there was no necklace, why did she want to go back up to Samcheonggak?"

"You got me," I said.

She turned and waved goodbye to us, a cheery smile on her face. She reached into one of the pockets in her khaki jungle jacket, grabbed something, and held it up over her head. It was small, black, and cylindrical.

"Oh, for Christ's sake," Ernie said. "A roll of goddamn film. She must've shot more than one."

"And left the best one hidden up there."

"But she promised," Ernie whined.

"She promised that she wouldn't use the film that had already been confiscated by the KNPs," I said. "But she specifically stated that anything shot before or after that was hers and fair game for publication."

"She tricked us," Ernie said, incredulity in his voice.

Katie Byrd Worthington climbed into the back seat of the cab. We watched as it sped off. We were blocked from following by about thirty jammed-in kimchi cabs and a herd of traffic flowing in front of us.

"We could go over to the Bando," Ernie said. "Find her there."

"Wouldn't do any good. She'll ship that film to Hong Kong before she's back in her hotel room."

"I wonder what's on it."

"We'll find out soon enough."

"Yeah," Ernie agreed. "In Sunday's edition of the *Oversexed Observer*. I can hardly wait till Colonel Brace gets a look."

"Yeah. He'll be delighted."

We approached the back gate of Yongsan Compound and sensed immediately that something was wrong. Crossed metal stanchions blocked vehicular traffic. Armed MPs in full combat regalia stood behind the barricade. We slowed and pulled up to the guard shack.

Ernie handed the MP our dispatch. "What the hell's going on?"

As he thumbed through the onion leaf, the MP said, "Alert."

"Focus Lens?" I asked.

"None other," he replied, handing the clipboard back to me. I slid it between the seats. "All personnel are to report to their duty stations," the MP said, "in full combat gear. The entire headquarters will be moving out at eighteen-hundred hours."

"That'll be a cluster," Ernie said.

The MP shrugged and waved us on. Two armed MPs dragged one of the stanchions backward, and we rolled onto the home compound of the 8th United States Army.

"What about Strange?" I said to Ernie.

"What about him?"

"He's still wallowing in a world of waste, having missed a day of work. And we don't know yet if he's been busted for the misappropriated document. How's this alert going to affect him?"

"Probably won't," Ernie said, turning left toward the barracks. "The Green Machine can go on alert and chew up GIs at the same time. It's had plenty of practice."

-7-

At the CID office, Staff Sergeant Riley was already loading equipment into the back of a three-quarter-ton truck. Miss Kim had been released to go home, as had all the Korean and American civilians who worked on base. This exercise would be strictly military, ostensibly designed to prove that even the bureaucratic staff of the 8th Army headquarters could shrug off their reliance on paper-pushing, at least temporarily, and become field soldiers again.

"About *time* you two got here," Riley said. "Load that field table in the back of the truck. And the teletype machine."

We'd be setting up a general purpose or "GP" tent, large enough to house an infantry squad of about ten people along with their cots and other gear. But instead of housing troops, it would serve as our in-the-field CID office. We'd have electric lights and communication equipment, folding wooden tables to use as desks, and hopefully the luxury of a diesel space heater and a functioning coffee urn.

Ernie and I did as we were told. For once. At least spending a few days in the field would allow us to stop making dumb black-market arrests and get our minds off troublemakers like Katie Byrd Worthington and Strange. Or at least, we thought it would. As we were loading the teletype machine, someone sneaked up behind us.

"Had any *strange* lately?" he asked.

Ernie and I both practically jumped out of our skin.

Strange grinned, wagging his empty plastic cigarette holder between thin lips, like some sort of demented FDR.

"Why are you sneaking up on us like that?" Ernie asked.

"Gotta keep a low profile," Strange said, glancing around. "Eyes everywhere."

He was dressed for combat: fatigues, steel pot, web gear with ammo pouches and canteen. The side of his skull was plastered with a gauze patch and his left arm was in a sling. Every one of his pudgy fingers was ringed with white tape. Still, he somehow managed to keep his shades firmly covering his eyes as he spoke.

"They released you from the One-Two-One," I said.

"Fifteen stitches," he said proudly. "No concussion."

"Your head must be pretty hard," Ernie said.

Strange frowned.

"With the way Major Cranston was ranting on and on," I said, "we figured you'd be locked up by now."

"Him? He's full of BS. Acts tough but he's a wuss. Doesn't

want the Classified Documents cage to be embarrassed by the NCO-in-charge going AWOL, even for only a day. Orting slipped the document back in place so nobody noticed it had been missing. Then I fed Major Cranston a bullshit story about a traffic accident and being knocked out and ending up in a Korean hospital. He pretended to buy it and I pretended to be sorry, so now we're back to business as usual. Besides, if I'm locked up, you two will be locked up with me."

Ernie froze. Slowly, he finished setting the teletype machine on the bed of the truck, dusted his hands, and stepped toward Sergeant First Class Harvey. He grabbed both his fatigue lapels in his clenched fists. "What the *hell* are you talking about?"

Strange's cigarette holder bounced as he sputtered.

"Hey, let go of the material," he said.

"Talk," Ernie said.

"I mean, you guys knew about the top-secret document. You transported it for me, gave it to Orting."

"Yeah, so?"

"You're law enforcement officers. If you come across a misappropriated classified document, you're supposed to turn it in. Report it."

The muscles in Ernie's forearms clenched and he lifted Strange so high off the ground that the tips of his combat boots barely touched the ground.

"You'd rat *us* out? After we saved your fat butt and did you a favor?"

Strange's cheeks bulged, and I wondered whether he was gulping down enough air. Still, he managed to squeak out a reply."Well, I haven't yet."

"But you *will*?"

"I didn't say that. It depends."

"Depends on what?"

"If you let go of me, for one."

Ernie breathed heavily. I knew he wanted nothing more than to punch Strange right across his quivering chops, and honestly, I wouldn't have minded if he did. While Ernie thought it over, I decided to intervene.

"What the hell's going on here, Strange?" I asked. "What are you trying to pull?"

"The name's Harvey," he pleaded, in an even higher pitch now. Ernie still hadn't released his grip.

I patted Ernie on the shoulder. "Let him go," I said. "Let him talk for a minute. Then we can pummel him if he doesn't have a good explanation."

Reluctantly, Ernie lowered Strange to the ground.

Sergeant First Class Harvey made a big show of straightening his field gear and the fatigue shirt beneath it, then readjusting his dark glasses and tilting his steel pot back to a more horizontal angle.

"That's better," he said.

"Talk!" Ernie yelled.

Startled, Strange finally started moving his mouth. At first it was just incoherent babbling, but then, just as he was getting to the point about what he wanted us to do, Staff Sergeant Riley emerged from the CID office and started shouting at us for not loading fast enough.

"We still have way too much crap in here! Field desks and cots and the GP tent with the poles and the stakes and the ropes. They're not going to move themselves."

Before Ernie could tell him what he could do with all that stuff, I shouted back, "We're on it, Sarge. Be right there."

Apparently mollified, he reentered the building.

"So let me get this straight," Ernie said, turning back to Strange. "You want us to help you find this North Korean girlfriend of yours, and if we don't, you're gonna turn us in for improper handling of a top-secret document."

"You make it sound too transactional," Strange replied.

Ernie breathed down on him, their noses almost touching. "How *should* it sound?"

"Like you're willing to help me, in return for all the things I've done for you."

I stepped between them. "If you turn us in for mishandling a classified document," I said, "you'll be burned yourself."

"I don't care. She's in danger, and saving her is all that matters to me."

Ernie rolled his eyes.

"What's her name?" I asked.

"Kim Yoon-jeong," he said.

"Any relation to the Great Leader?" Ernie asked.

"No. Her *songbun* was low."

"Her what?" Ernie asked.

"*Songbun*," Strange answered. "Her rating in the Communist system. Her family was descended from a landlord class, so they were considered untrustworthy. That's why they had to live in the outskirts of Hamhung, so far from Pyongyang."

Pyongyang was the capital of North Korea, and only the anointed elites in the Great Leader's caste system were allowed to live there.

"She escaped from North Korea," I said quietly. "Didn't she?"

"Yes. Along with her family."

"But if she hated North Korea enough to risk her life trying to get away, why did she ask for the document?"

"She had no choice. They found her oldest son, Jong-hyuk, kidnapped him, and told her she had to convince me to steal the document for her. They promised her they would keep it for just a few hours, and I could take the document back to the cage the next morning and no one would be the wiser."

"They were grooming you as a source," Ernie said.

Strange shrugged. "What choice did I have?"

"You should've blown the whistle right then."

Strange spread his fingers. "They had her son. She was panicked and crying. What was I supposed to do, spit in her face?"

"Better than what you did."

"Why'd they lock you up?"

"When she was late in returning the document, I became nervous and went looking for her."

"At the *nakji* house?"

"Yeah. That's where Shin operates."

"He's the leader of this operation?"

"I don't know if he's the leader, but he's some sort of go-between."

That explained why he'd provided us such a precise map. He wanted to make sure we were in exactly the right spot when he ordered his boys to descend on us. And by then they'd already returned the boy to the custody of his grandmother.

Strange continued. "Shin told me to wait, that it was taking longer than they'd expected. I started cursing him out, and he and his boys knocked me around a little, then dragged me downstairs into that cage."

"But when we found you," I said, "you had the document in your possession."

"Yeah. After you two left the *nakji* house, Shin gave it to me. He told me to make sure it was returned to the classified documents vault."

"They didn't want Eighth Army to know it had been missing?" I asked.

"No."

"So why didn't he let you go then?" Ernie asked.

"Because you guys were in the neighborhood. He wanted to wait until things quieted down."

"Until they did to us what they do to the fresh squid," Ernie said.

I winced and turned to Strange. "And you haven't seen your girlfriend since?"

"She's not my girlfriend," he said. "I'm just worried about her."

"You oughta be," Ernie said.

"What do you mean?" Strange asked.

"Those boys play rough."

Strange stared at him for a moment and then said, "That's why I'm here. I want you guys to go out to Itaewon and help me find her."

"At the moment," I said, "we're preoccupied."

Ernie and I turned back to the task at hand, which was loading the GP tent and once we were on the far side of the truck, we murmured between ourselves.

"She's using him," Ernie said.

"Of course she is. But if we play our cards right, we might be able to nab not only her, but the agents behind her."

"Strange could go to jail."

"So could we if we do nothing and this gets out."

"Why not just turn the whole thing over to counter-intel?"

"I think we're in a little too deep for that."

Ernie nodded in silent agreement.

The heavy canvas tent was folded like a gigantic hot dog bun. We dragged it into position and then tilted part of it against the back of the truck. Ernie climbed up onto the truck bed and got ready to pull while I lifted.

"On three," I said. "One, two, *three!*"

The canvas barely moved. Strange hurried up and grabbed hold of the side opposite me.

"Okay. Again," I said. "One, two, *three!*"

This time we got it partway up. We continued to count and hoist and heave and tug until the bulk of the canvas was inside lying flat in the center of the truck. As we loaded the poles and the stakes and the ropes, it hit me what we should do. Ernie hopped down from the back of the truck, and we stepped aside out of earshot from Strange.

"Strange is right," I said. "We could land in hot water just for giving the document to Orting and not reporting the misappropriation immediately."

Ernie turned toward Strange and growled. "I'll kill him."

"This isn't necessarily a counter-intel case," I continued. "We don't know what this woman's motives are, or what the guys who imprisoned Strange are up to. Best if we investigate first, then take action."

"And bust it wide open," Ernie said. "Then nobody will give a shit about anyone passing a document along to an unauthorized person without permission."

"Right. And Strange won't land in the stockade either."

Ernie glared at Strange. "Not at the top of my list right now, but fine. What do we do?"

"When the headquarters moves out, we accompany Strange to Itaewon. Find this North Korean girlfriend. Interrogate her. Maybe convince her to turn the other guys over to us."

"I'd just as soon beat the crap out of him for getting us into this mess."

I patted Ernie on the shoulder. "Maybe later. And I'll help."

Early that evening, we accompanied Strange to Itaewon, walked past the eatery marked with *nakji*, and entered the gate of the hooch where we'd seen the mother and the three children of the mysterious North Korean woman. There was no light on in the hooch. Strange stepped up onto the wooden porch, slid the oil-paper door back, and flipped the switch. A single bulb burned brightly overhead. The room was completely deserted. Not a stick of furniture or a scrap of clothing.

Suddenly, a diminutive Korean woman appeared behind us.

"They go," she said in English.

I turned and asked her who she was. She explained that she was the owner of this small complex of hooches. She and her husband lived in the one at the end.

"Where'd they go?" I asked.

She shook her head. They hadn't told her. They'd been in a hurry: two men with a handcart had arrived, and the family had loaded up and departed all within a few minutes.

"When did this happen?"

"This morning."

Strange sat on the wooden porch, head lolling forward. Suddenly, both hands were on his face, and his narrow shoulders began to heave. The old woman retreated. To give him some privacy, Ernie and I stepped through the gate and out into the roadway.

"An old story," Ernie said. "He got played, and then she dumped him."

"After getting what she wanted."

"Yeah," Ernie agreed, "but why?"

"He's clearly not her type."

"No. I mean why'd she want that document about Focus Lens?"

"She wanted it because they'd kidnapped her son."

"That might've been a ploy," Ernie said, "to put pressure on Strange."

"Maybe," I agreed. "But if she is really cooperating with North Korean agents, she'd stick around and work him and trick him into bringing out more classified information. Or maybe we're wrong about the whole North Korean agent thing and she's just some sort of sadist trying to land him in trouble."

"I don't think so," Ernie replied. "I think we'll find out soon enough who these guys were and what they wanted that document for."

"How will we find that out?"

"The same way we find out most things—the hard way.

They'll take some sort of action and somebody will investigate and we'll be left holding the bag."

"Unless we can head them off somehow."

Wiping his eyes, Strange joined us and we trudged back toward the main drag. On the way, we took a closer look at the *nakji* house. It was now boarded up and deserted. Even the bulb inside the sign had been taken out.

"Squidless," Ernie said.

"Bereft of octopi," I added.

Strange didn't think any of it was funny.

Ernie and I spent the next two hours driving toward the temporary field headquarters of the 8th United States Army. In the back of the jeep, we'd piled our extra field gear like sleeping bags—or in GI parlance "fart sacks"—along with a duffel bag filled with extra wet-weather gear. The Air Force meteorological office predicted a storm front moving in later that night.

Strange was wedged between two duffel bags, eyes still red from crying. Or I imagined they were red since I couldn't see them beneath the shades. We were about a half-hour outside Seoul on a country road, winding our way through the western edge of the Taebaek Mountains. Finally, he spoke.

"You two probably think I'm sweet on her."

"Sweet on who?" Ernie asked, all innocence.

"Kim Yoon-jeong." He paused. "You know, a few years ago,

her husband was murdered by a local commissar in Ham-hung, her hometown."

"Why?"

"Because he refused to shortchange the workers in the local fisheries collective and pass the profits along to the party bosses. Yoon-ah decided that—"

"Who?"

"Yoon-jeong. Yoon-ah's my nickname for her."

"Pretty intimate, eh?" Ernie said.

Strange frowned. "You wanna hear the story or not?"

"Go ahead," I prompted.

"So Yoon-jeong knew that she and her family better get out of Dodge, and fast. But there's no disappearing in North Korea. You need permits for everything. To move from one apartment to another, even to buy a train ticket. So she convinced one of the local fishermen to allow her and her mother and her three kids to travel with them to sea."

"They must have inspections in port," I said, "before the fishing boats leave."

"You better believe they do," Strange said.

"So how did she get past that?"

"The storage hold. Full of ice to be chopped up and preserve the catch once they start taking on fish. She and her family carved out little caverns in the bottoms of the big blocks. She held on to the baby, and she and her mother and the two kids lay down while the fishermen dropped canvas and then straw mats on top, nice and cozy like, along with rubber tubes so they could breathe. Then they fitted the ice over her. When the inspectors came aboard, they looked around, but they didn't lift up the blocks. Both the baby and the smallest girl were almost dead by the time the fishermen made it out to the open sea and finally pulled Yoon-ah and her family out of the hold, but everybody eventually recovered."

"And they sailed toward South Korea?"

"Yeah. Slipping past ROK Navy patrol boats in the middle of the night. Eventually the ship made it to shore and let them off at an old broken-down pier."

"And the fishermen?"

"She's not sure what happened to them. But she hopes they made it back to international waters, continued their fishing, and eventually returned to Hamhung with a hold full of seafood."

"But she doesn't know."

"She never will."

Ernie leaned forward on the steering wheel, flashed his bright lights, and then stepped on the gas and swerved around a slow-moving convoy of ROK Army trucks.

"So why'd these North Korean fishermen risk their lives just for this Yoon and her family?"

"Because her late husband had risked his life for them. On more than one occasion. She tells me that people up there never talk about it because they're afraid, but there's a silent resistance to the government, conducted by like-minded people almost as if by telepathy. They don't do anything revolutionary, exactly, nothing that directly opposes the government. They just look out for one another."

"Based on old family ties?" I asked.

"Yeah. Some of those people have been in the same fishing villages since way before the Korean War. Generations before."

"So she made it to freedom," Ernie said.

"Yes. Once she left that pier, she and her family surrendered themselves at the first KNP station they found." The Korean National Police. "After a few months of debriefing and rehabilitation, they were allowed to enter South Korean society."

"And then she met you."

"That's right."

"What a setback," Ernie said.

-8-

The alert had been called on a Friday, and by Saturday out at the new base camp, everybody was grousing about having to set up tents and suffer the intermittent rain and put up with the long cold nights when we should've been enjoying a weekend in the neon-spangled environs of Itaewon's nightclub district. Instead, with each step, we were forced to hoist rubberized overshoes out of sucking muck. To top it off, Ernie and I had landed the extra duty of the midnight-to-four perimeter guard.

Just when we thought things couldn't get worse, they did. Saturday afternoon, Staff Sergeant Riley found us in the mess tent, standing at a five-foot-high feeding table and shoveling something resembling mashed potatoes and meatloaf into our mouths.

"Chief of Staff wants to talk to you two," he said. "Now!"

Ernie finished the last of his spuds, chewed, swallowed, and said, "What'd we do?"

"It's what you *didn't* do."

"Like?"

"You'll find out when you get there."

With a wad of bread, I wiped the last bit of gravy out of my mess kit, wishing the flaccid white dough were a wedge of tortilla de maiz and the gravy were a dollop of pico de gallo. Shoving such wistfulness out of my mind, I dropped my spoon inside the metal kit, fit the two sides together, and clicked shut the clasp. There were big corrugated drums of hot soapy dish water outside with wooden-handled wire brushes and a couple of tubs of rinse water beyond that, but there was so much crud already floating in the insipid fluid that I decided I'd clean my eating utensils later. Hooking it back to my web belt, I told Riley, "That's a lot of rank to be talking to a couple of low-level schmucks like us. Wouldn't the Provost Marshal want to talk to us first?"

"He's there. With the Chief of Staff. Waiting on your sorry butts."

On the walk over, Ernie said, "Knock off the crap, Riley. What in the hell is this about?"

"It's about your girlfriend."

"Which one?"

"The one whose camera you were supposed to confiscate and stomp on."

Katie Byrd Worthington.

Riley continued, "Somebody got ahold of an advance copy of tomorrow's issue of the *Oversexed Observer*."

Ernie groaned.

I did too, inwardly, feeling the noxious mess hall meal bubble ominously at the base of my esophagus.

We were made to wait outside the command tent for about twenty minutes. I spent the time using a stick to wedge crusted mud out from the ridged soles of my combat boots. Finally, a female lieutenant peeked through canvas flaps and motioned for us to enter. We did. Naked bulbs were strung from rafters, and the flooring was an expanse of wooden pallets. In the center on a metal folding chair sat Brigadier General Hubert N. Frankenton, Chief of Staff of the 8th United States Army. Protecting him like a barricade was a long green field table stacked with various documents and folders and three-ring binders. Our boss, Colonel Walter P. Brace, 8th Army's Provost Marshal, somberly slid some of the paperwork toward the Chief of Staff.

Ernie and I were about to salute when General Frankenton—the man Katie Byrd Worthington called "Frankie Baby"—motioned for us to take a seat. We did, angling our chairs toward the two men.

"Tomorrow's news today," General Frankenton said, and slid an advance copy of the *Overseas Observer* across the tabletop.

Ernie and I studied the front page. To our surprise, there

was no semi-nude photo of General Frankenton. Instead, a group of female soldiers was arrayed in front of an antiaircraft gun, glaring at the camera and giving the finger to a huge red-and-white cloverleaf patch—the symbol of the 8th United States Army.

The headline blared: WAR WOMEN.

The byline, as expected, said Katie Byrd Worthington.

I started to read the article, but General Frankenton interrupted and said, "Do you know where that bitch is?"

Ernie and I looked at each other. Then I turned to the general.

"She keeps a room at the Bando Hotel," I said, "in downtown Seoul."

Colonel Brace broke in, "We've already searched there, sent an MP patrol over this morning. They say she checked out yesterday."

"No forwarding address?"

"None."

Ernie and I exchanged another glance, shrugged, and then I said, "No idea, sir."

He studied us. "Do you think you could find her?"

Again, like Laurel and Hardy, Ernie and I gaped at each other. And once again, Ernie let me speak. Although I almost expected him to grimace and rub the top of his head.

"I suppose so, sir," I answered. "How quickly, I'm not sure."

General Frankenton had grown impatient. He checked his

wristwatch. "How about by twenty-two hundred hours? You will find her skinny little ass, slap her in handcuffs, and have her thrown into the Yongsan Compound lockup before midnight? Does that sound doable?"

I gulped. He didn't wait for an answer.

"We're pulling this rag off the shelves of the PX." He leaned forward, snatched the newspaper out of my hands, and then raised the loose pulp of the *Overseas Observer* and shook it in the air. "Not one military base in this command will be selling this tomorrow. I might catch hell from some bleeding-heart congressman or those blood-sucking civil liberty lawyers at the ACLU but, frankly, I don't give a shit. A story like this"— he flicked the paper with his forefinger—"is detrimental to the good order and discipline of the Eighth United States Army. And right now, those North Korean sons of bitches are watching our every move. They hate these joint South Korean–US exercises, and they hate them with a passion. They claim that Focus Lens is '*provocative.*'" He paused for a breath. "Provocative, my ass. Them having seven hundred thousand soldiers massed along with artillery and battalion after battalion of tanks shoved right up along the DMZ, *that's* provocative. Not us. We're just trying to make sure that, if and when the time comes, we can defend this goddamn country from their Commie aggression. And then this . . . this . . ." He struggled for the word. Finally it erupted out of his mouth. "This *bitch* comes along and tries to destroy the cohesiveness of our forces by *lying* about a few rapes and assaults that have already been properly dealt with."

Rapes and assaults? Neither Ernie nor I knew what he was talking about.

"So you two," General Frankenton said, "you don't just have to *try* to find her. You have to get your asses in gear and find her *tonight*. Take her into custody." He waved both hands in the air. "I don't care how you do it, just *do* it. And then I want her held at the Yongsan Compound MP Station, like I said, until I have time to go down there and explain the facts of life to her."

Katie Byrd Worthington was a civilian. Her legal fate fell well outside of 8th Army's jurisdiction. The US military could pull her press pass and deny her access to our bases—if we had justification—but arresting her would be strictly illegal. Illegal not only under American law, but also Korean law. Colonel Brace, who knew this only too well, remained silent.

General Frankenton seemed to be reading our minds. "Oh, I know what you're thinking. You'll get in hot water for arresting a civilian. So use that buddy of yours downtown. That Korean cop who's always asking for your help. What's his name?"

"Mr. Kill," I said.

"Yeah, him. Just tell him I don't want this Katie Byrd broad getting murdered. Not yet, anyway." He looked back and forth between us. "Any questions?"

Ernie remained quiet. He'd been in the army long enough to know better than to mouth off to someone as powerful as the Chief of Staff of the 8th United States Army, even when he was issuing an illegal order. General Frankenton glared at us. Searching, I thought, for any hint of insurrection.

Finally, I said, "No questions, sir."

"Good. Take this piece of shit," he said, shoving the copy of the *Overseas Observer* back toward us. "And when you find this skinny-ass so-called reporter, you notify my adjutant immediately. Is that understood?"

"Understood, sir."

He flicked his wrist, and we were dismissed.

"Is he out of his *freaking* mind?" Ernie asked.

We were in the jeep, our gear already loaded in the back, driving through lengthening shadows on the narrow country road heading west toward Seoul. A convoy of ROK Army tanks approached, the girth of the massive war machines so wide that they enveloped most of the blacktop. Ernie pulled to safety on the side of the road, stopped, and turned off the jeep's engine.

As the armored behemoths rumbled past us, he said, "If we arrest Katie Byrd, we could go to prison. It's a federal offense."

"Even if he ordered us to do it?"

"Even if. It's a crime to carry out an illegal order."

"I don't remember them teaching us that in Basic Training."

"It's not something the army likes to advertise."

They also don't teach American soldiers about the Nuremberg trials after World War II, where the legal precedent was established that saying, "I was just following orders," wasn't a valid defense.

"So we're in a bind," I said. "But look at the bright side. At least we got out of the midnight-to-four perimeter guard."

Ernie thought about it. "There's that."

"Do you think we should notify the base camp security officer that we won't be there tonight?"

"Nah. He'll figure it out when we don't show."

The last tank in the convoy passed by, and the thunder of the iron treads faded into blissful silence. A magpie flitted across the road. Ernie started the jeep's engine again and pulled back out onto pavement. We drove through winding mountain passes toward the glimmering twilight that hovered above my own personal Oz: what I thought of as the Emerald City of Seoul.

Ten minutes later, Ernie asked, "Did you read that article yet?"

"I can't now. I get carsick."

"This isn't a car, it's a jeep."

"Even worse." The independent suspension in jeeps meant that they wobbled more than regular cars, or so it seemed to me.

"So what did old Katie Byrd come up with that pissed off Frankie Baby so much?"

"Whatever it is, it's worse than being caught half-naked dancing with a bunch of *kisaeng.*"

"I wouldn't mind if she put a picture like that of me in the newspaper."

"Nobody gives a shit if *you're* dancing with *kisaeng.*"

"They do too."

"Who does?"

"The *kisaeng.* They like me."

"How do you know?"

"They tell me so."

"They say that to every customer."

"They laugh at my jokes."

"They probably don't even understand your jokes."

"You're bursting my bubble."

"Don't cry."

"I'll try not to."

I pulled the *Overseas Observer* out of my jacket pocket, unfolded it, and began to read.

"Pull over," I told Ernie, "in case I have to barf."

"Go ahead and barf. I'll just hose it down when we get to the motor pool."

It was dark enough now that I had to use a flashlight to read the article. As we rolled ever closer to the outskirts of Seoul, Ernie asked, "What does it say?"

"Katie Byrd really outdid herself with this one."

"Apparently."

"It's about this transportation unit. They have a lot of female soldiers. You know, because technically they're not a combat unit."

"Unless they get shot at."

"Right. They function along the DMZ, and in an actual war-footing situation, they would perform close support to various combat units. Like that antiaircraft battery that Katie Byrd had them pose in front of."

"They look like tough broads."

"They oughta be. According to the article, they spend more than half their time out in the field doing various combat support operations. River crossing, mostly."

"Across the Imjin?"

"Yes."

Ernie whistled. The Imjin River flows south out of North Korea, crosses the Military Demarcation Line, and then runs parallel to the DMZ west toward the Yellow Sea. It's known for its narrow channels, rapid currents, and frigid water. Water that's close to freezing even during the summertime, since it's composed mostly of mountainous ice-melt.

"If you fall off that river-crossing barge into the Imjin," Ernie said, "you're toast. Even Mark Spitz would be dragged under."

No matter how good a swimmer you are, when your body temperature plunges and you're being pulled down and around and backward by colliding currents, nobody expects you to last more than a few seconds in the turbulent waters of the Imjin.

"So what's their beef?" Ernie asked.

"According to the article, they're being sexually assaulted."

"How serious?"

"Very," I told him. "One of them was beaten and raped. Ended up at the 121 Evac. Her injuries were so severe that she was shipped off to Tripler Medical in Hawaii. She's still there, according to this."

Ernie whistled. "How come we never heard about it?"

"You got me." When the brass wants to keep something quiet, they classify the incident as confidential, and it doesn't appear amongst our regular crime reports.

"So was somebody arrested?"

"An attacker was identified, but according to Katie Byrd, the army claims there's not enough evidence to charge him with anything."

"The old consensual sex thing?"

"Yeah. Apparently, she gave her consent for him to beat the crap out of her."

"Typical," Ernie said.

"Sure."

"Are the attacks still going on?"

"Not anymore. According to this, these war women don't go anywhere alone, and they arm themselves. If not with rifles, with bayonets and clubs and mace."

"Mace is illegal in the army."

"Don't I know it. Like your switchblade and your brass knuckles."

"That's different. I'm in law enforcement."

We crossed the slow-flowing Han River, which led us into the environs of Seoul. After passing Walker Hill on our right, Ernie followed Hangang Road, until he swerved north toward Dongbinggo, and shortly thereafter we reached our destination of Yongsan Compound.

"First we change out of these monkey suits," Ernie said, meaning our combat fatigues. "Then we head down to the Bando to find Katie Byrd."

"General Frankenton said she checked out."

"Which meant that she planned on going somewhere."

"Where?"

"We're about to find out."

"If the MPs couldn't beat a forwarding address out of the Bando Hotel staff, what makes you think we can?"

"Brains," Ernie said.

"Whose brains?"

"Yours," he told me.

"Mine?"

"Yeah. I'm sure you'll think of something."

About five minutes later, I did.

-9-

"Call her main office in Hong Kong?" Ernie asked.

"Why not?" I replied. "The number's right here on the masthead of the *Overseas Observer*."

"The what?"

"The masthead. It gives the name and address and other contact information for the newspaper. And who the publisher is and all that stuff."

"You think they'll authorize an AUTOVON call for that?"

"Of course they will. This is General Frankenton's hot project."

AUTOVON was the system the military had for monitoring overseas calls made from military phones. Permission had to be requested and granted first and then an authorization number would be issued that allowed the overseas operator to patch the call through.

Yongsan Compound was mostly deserted. There was only a skeleton crew to provide security and communications support. We stopped in the barracks, took a quick but welcome shower, and changed into our running-the-ville outfits, complete with nylon jackets.

At the MP station, the desk sergeant hesitated when I told him we needed an AUTOVON number.

"Lieutenant Gladstone will have to authorize that."

"Fine. Where is he?"

"He went to chow."

"Well, tell him to un-go to chow," Ernie said. "This is a top-priority investigation, direct from the Chief of Staff."

"*You* tell him to un-go to chow," the desk sergeant replied.

"Fine. Which mess hall did he go to?"

There was more than one on the massive 8th Army headquarters compound. But since over ninety percent of the GIs were out in the field, most of the mess halls were closed. The desk sergeant started to reply when a clerk in wrinkled fatigues appeared from a back room. He held a pink phone message slip in his hands. He looked at it and squinted.

"Either one of you guys, Sween-o?"

"Sueño," I said. "That's me."

He handed the phone message to me. "Who is this broad, calls herself Katie Byrd?"

"She's a reporter," I said.

"Well, she's one rude b—" He caught himself. "Person. Demanded that I leave the MP station and find you, even though I told her we're short-staffed and I couldn't leave."

"When did you talk to her?"

"Just a minute ago," he said.

"Did she hang up?"

"I hung up on her." He stroked his chin. "I never knew a woman could cuss like that."

"She's a country girl," Ernie offered.

The clerk looked at him, puzzled. "Oh," he said, and left through the same back door from which he'd entered.

I grabbed the extra phone at the end of the MP Desk and spoke to the operator, telling her I needed an outside line here in Seoul. She didn't quibble, since in-country local calls don't require AUTOVON authorization. I recited the number to her, and about thirty seconds later, after a series of buzzes and clicks, the phone was ringing. Somebody snatched it up.

"Sueño? Is that you?" Unmistakeably Katie Byrd Worthington's voice.

"It's me all right," I said.

"What took you so long to call me back?"

"You caught me sunbathing," I said.

"Well, wipe that greasy lotion off and get your ass in gear."

"Why?"

"You've got a mission, buddy. Approved by General Frankenton himself."

"Yeah," I told her. "I've got a mission all right. My mission is to lock you up."

"Frankie Baby told me about that. But your mission has changed."

"'Changed?'"

"What, did I stutter? I just talked to the old boy. He wants you and your sidekick Ernie to pick me up and transport me to somewhere called Wonju, southeast of here. There, we meet someone who'll escort us to the current position of Charley Company of the 877th Field Transportation Battalion. You got all that?"

"Bull."

"'Bull' you don't got it, or 'bull' you don't believe it?"

"Both. Why *should* I believe you?"

"Don't. Frankie Baby said if you have any questions to call his adjutant. He'll confirm. Do it now. I can't wait here all day."

"Where are you?"

"Itaewon. Where else? For once, there are no obnoxious GIs hanging around."

"Yeah. All the obnoxious GIs are in the field. Only us gentlemanly types are left."

She snorted, told me where she was waiting, and hung up.

"Lieutenant Gladstone just returned," the MP desk sergeant said. "You can get that AUTOVON number now."

"The situation has changed. We won't need it."

Downstairs in the MP Arms Room, Ernie and I turned our rifles into the on-duty armorer. Then I checked out a .45 automatic, ammunition, and a leather shoulder holster.

"You expecting trouble?" Ernie asked.

"We're picking up Katie Byrd," I told him.

"Oh." He checked out a pistol too. After he signed for it, he seemed to ponder something.

"What?" I asked.

"Maybe we should check out a bazooka."

"For little old Katie Byrd?"

"She's the most dangerous woman I ever met."

When we found her sitting at the bar at the King Club, she didn't bother to greet us, but just slid over a glossy eight-by-ten photograph. Ernie and I gaped down at the photo, twisting it to catch more of the dim red light above the bar.

"Christ," Ernie said. "A middle-aged man taking off *all* his clothes?"

"Along with the *kisaeng*," I added.

"Yeah," Ernie replied. "But she's young and has a figure. He looks like a blimp."

"Nothing like a half-quart of Jack Daniels to loosen you up a little," Katie Byrd added.

Before we left the MP station, I called General Frankenton's adjutant, who confirmed that our mission had changed. Instead of locking her up, we were now supposed to escort *Overseas Observer* reporter Katie Byrd Worthington to wherever Charley Company of the 877th Field Transportation Battalion were currently operating. She was to be allowed full access to the female soldiers and when she was done, we were to escort her back to Seoul. Apparently, 8th Army's strategy on how to handle this bad publicity had done a one-eighty.

"This is the *clean* photo," Katie added. "After this, he starts getting raunchy with a pair of chopsticks."

"What'd he do with those?" Ernie said.

"Don't ask. It's all on that roll of film you two helped me retrieve from Samcheong whatever-that-place-is-called."

"You tricked us," Ernie said.

"Oh, *boo-hoo*. The fact of the matter is that I did lose my grandma's necklace. Not there, but somewhere else. I'll find it one day."

"But the real reason you wanted to go up there was to retrieve your film."

"Hey, it's worth its weight in gold. Frankie Baby now knows that the entire roll and every photo on it is sitting in the possession of our main office in Hong Kong, and we can publish any photo we want whenever we want."

"You've got him by the balls."

"Crudely put, but yes. The first roll showed him dancing around shirtless with a bunch of young chicks, which is embarrassing enough. But this roll shows him actually having sexual relations with one of those women, a court-martial offense for any married US Army officer."

"Career-ending," Ernie said.

"You better believe it," Katie said. "Adultery is one of the umpteen deadly sins in the Uniform Code of Military Justice.

Now that he knows I have the goods, Frankie Baby's about to shit a brick, which is why he authorized you to escort me to good old Charley Company to continue this little investigation of mine."

"A story about a demonstration and work stoppage by female soldiers will make him look bad too," I said.

"Yes. But not as bad as those photos."

She was right. Although any rational person would believe that failing to protect your own troops from sexual assault was worse than being embarrassed by some nude photographs taken during a drunken orgy, the first was survivable for General Frankenton's career and the second wasn't. If these photos were revealed, there would be such an uproar back in the States that Frankenton would be relieved of his command, forced to retire, and possibly even court-martialed on the way out of service. However, accusations of sexual assault were always negotiable. The perpetrators denied, the bosses rationalized, and the women were left to fend for themselves.

Katie Byrd's exposé might not even be picked up by the major wire services, *United Press International* or the *Associated Press*. He-said-she-said stories happen every day of the week. And in much of the American heartland, it's seen as unpatriotic to bad-mouth our boys overseas. Most people don't even realize that our girls are serving overseas also. Right alongside them.

Katie Byrd finished the last of her beer, slapped a few *won* on the bar, stood up, hoisted her canvas camera bag over her shoulder, and said, "You ready to roll?"

"We are. Are you?"

"Ready."

Ernie studied her. "What, no overnight bag? No makeup kit? You're not even bringing a change of panties?"

"No," Katie replied. "Are you?"

I couldn't help but laugh and then stifled it when Ernie aimed his evil stare at me. Awkwardly, the three of us walked outside toward the jeep.

Wonju is the largest city in the province of Gangwon, which is situated near the center of South Korea's east coast. As such, it's a hub for military activity, mainly defensive. US and Korean military intelligence had long established that North Korean invasion plans included more than just a massive armor and infantry push southward along the DMZ. They also included amphibious assaults on both the western and eastern coasts of the Korean Peninsula. It was said that the North Koreans had hundreds, if not thousands, of small, swift assault boats, each capable of carrying about a half-dozen well-trained commandos. Their job would be to attack every target of opportunity they could find, including not just military bases but also police stations and city government installations, along with infrastructure: electrical power grids, telephone circuits, bridges, dams; anything that would disrupt the daily life of South Koreans and inhibit their ability to respond to external threats.

In the past, North Korean commando units had in fact invaded the east coast, hoping to inspire local villagers to rise up against the Americans and the Park Chung-hee regime. What had actually happened was that South Korean civilians risked their lives to turn them in, and in short order, the Communist intruders were massacred, though I doubted you'd ever hear that story in North Korea.

It was about midnight when we arrived at Camp Long near Wonju. We checked with the Staff Duty Officer at the base headquarters building, but no one from Charley Company had reported in. We decided to wait outside in the jeep. Katie snuggled up between the sleeping bags we had brought, and Ernie and I sat in front, dozing. Occasionally, Ernie started the engine and let the heater pump out a little warm air.

It must've been about 2 A.M. when light shone in my eyes.

"You Sueño?" a female voice said.

"Yeah," I replied, shielding my eyes from the glare. "How about aiming that flashlight elsewhere?"

She did.

"Where's the reporter?" she asked.

I jabbed my thumb toward the back.

"Good. We'll take her from here."

By now, Ernie was awake and climbing out of the jeep. Katie

continued snoring. The woman with the flashlight reached in back and shook her awake.

"Ms. Worthington?"

Groggily, Katie nodded.

"We're here to take you to the unit. Show you what's going on."

"Oh, okay," Katie said, surprised, rubbing her eyes.

I climbed out of the jeep, and Katie followed. As she was gathering up her camera bag, I studied the woman in front of me. She was a husky gal, and tall, about five-eight. She was wearing fatigues and full combat gear, including a web belt with a pistol at her side. Her name tag said Hurley, and her rank was corporal.

"She stays with us," I told her. "In our jeep. We follow, and you lead us to your unit."

"No," she replied. "We don't need you."

Behind her, leaning against the wooden side slats in the bed of a three-quarter-ton truck were two more female soldiers. Casually, they balanced their M16 rifles on top of the slats.

"It's not a matter of whether or not you need us," Ernie said. "We were ordered to escort her to and from your unit, and that's what we're going to do."

The two women in the truck crouched slightly and leveled their weapons, aiming them directly at Ernie and me.

"I said," Corporal Hurley repeated slowly, "we don't need you."

Alert now, Katie sensed the standoff. "Settle down, boys," she said. "I'll be fine with these ladies. You just wait here on base, get yourselves a comfy room over at billeting. I'll meet you right here at the end of the day. About seventeen hundred hours." Five P.M. She glanced at Corporal Hurley. "Will that be enough time?"

"Plenty."

"Okay," Katie said, "then it's all set."

"She doesn't leave without us," Ernie repeated.

Katie shook her head. "Talk some sense into him, Sueño. This story is about these women. I don't need a couple of lunk-headed men tagging along."

"You travel with us, Katie. Those are our orders."

"Orders, schmorders. Frankie Baby won't mind. Are you forgetting our little photo shoot?"

She started to walk toward the truck, Hurley backing up with her.

I stepped forward. "I said *no*, Katie."

A rifle shot sounded. The round kicked up a cloud of dust and ricocheted off into the night. Ernie pulled his .45. I reached for mine. Apparently, Corporal Hurley was some sort of quick-draw artist.

Her .45 was already aimed directly at my head.

-10-

"She comes with *us*," Hurley said. "You want a shootout right here, we'll give you one."

Ernie and I were outgunned, not by Hurley's .45, but much more ominously by the two automatic military assault rifles manned by the two female sharpshooters standing on the bed of the truck in front of us.

"You'll regret this, Hurley."

"So will Eighth Army," she said, "if you try to stop us."

"*Ciao*," Katie Byrd said, turning then trotting across the tufted lawn. Without hesitation, she climbed into the cab of the truck. Hurley joined her, and after holstering her weapon, took a seat behind the steering wheel. The truck started up, backed out of the parking position, and turned in a wide arc toward the front gate of Camp Long. All the while, the two riflewomen in the back kept their assault weapons zeroed in on Ernie and me. As their taillights lit up to slow down before exiting the front gate, we both jumped into the jeep. Ernie started the engine, backed up, and followed at a distance.

We didn't have to talk about it. Katie Byrd Worthington had been assigned to us, and as far as the 8th Army brass was concerned, she was the most dangerous person on the Korean Peninsula. More dangerous in their minds than the Great Leader himself.

"They're trying to lose us," Ernie said, swinging the wheel in a maddening arc.

"You're like scabies," I told him. "Nobody can lose you, Ernie."

For some reason, he took it as a compliment. "You got that right."

Ernie would stay with them, of that I was sure, but whether or not we'd survive the effort was a different matter. I kept expecting them to take a pot shot at us since we were well within range, but so far they hadn't.

The little jeep tossed and turned across the rugged terrain. We were heading gradually uphill into the mountains, and on these dirt roads, there were few directional signs and less light. Eventually, we came to a railroad crossing with flashing bulbs ordering us to stop. Entering their glow felt, by contrast with the mountainous countryside surrounding us, as if we'd stopped at an intersection in downtown Manhattan.

"Where the hell is this unit bivouacked, anyway?" Ernie asked.

"Out in the boonies. The honchos try to make Focus Lens as realistic as possible. The North Koreans, in a real invasion, would be doing their best to land where our forces are most spread out."

The truck ahead of us swung around a jagged cliff to our right and then began up a steep incline. Ernie shoved the jeep into low gear and plowed forward, kicking up dust and gravel. At the crest of the ridge, we tilted downward precipitously for about a half-mile. Then the road leveled but wound back and forth like a harried serpent. Ahead, a whooshing sound grew louder.

"What the hell is that?" Ernie asked.

I listened for a second. "A river," I said.

"Rapids," Ernie replied. "Must be. Making all that racket."

Finally, the road straightened and after reaching the elevated bank of the rushing river, we turned left into a tree-lined darkness. Ahead, a single green light swung back and forth.

"What the hell's that?" Ernie said, squinting forward.

"A pendulum," I said, "above a pit."

"Oh, great. Just what I need. More of your literary bullshit."

Actually, it was two armed guards, waving a green lantern and ordering us to stop. As we approached, I realized that they were two young women, both in full combat gear, with M16 rifles trained on us.

Ernie came to a halt. "Can't you point those things somewhere else?" he asked.

"Dispatch," one of them said, holding out her free hand.

I handed her the clipboard with the onionskin attached, and she thumbed through it using a flashlight while her partner kept us covered. Finally, she tossed the dispatch back.

"Step out of the vehicle, both of you."

We did, keeping our hands in plain sight.

"We're going to take a little walk," she told us, "to the CP." The command post. "You'll keep your hands raised, and if you try anything funny, I'll shoot without further warning. Got it?"

"You're taking this war game pretty seriously, aren't you?" Ernie said.

She glared at him and said, "Keep it moving."

The command post was a GP tent about the size of half a volleyball court. We entered through the front flap, and inside, by the light of three or four hanging lanterns, we were frisked by a familiar face—Corporal Hurley. She removed our .45s, set them on a field table, and told the perimeter guard she could return to her post. Another lamp, this one yellow, provided an ambient glow. Katie Byrd sat perched on an army-issue cot, scribbling furiously in her notebook as another woman sat opposite her, both of them almost nose to nose. Now that the preliminaries were over, I could hear what they were saying.

"Every night?" Katie Byrd asked, incredulous. "They waited out by the latrine?"

"They're shits," the woman told her. "That's where they feel most at home."

"So if you had to urinate in the middle of the night, what would you do?"

"Piss in my canteen cup, usually. But if there were a few of us awake, we'd go out together, armed to the teeth, and protect one another as we each did our business."

"But if you weren't armed, and if you went to the latrine alone, what happened?"

"Gang bang," the woman said. "Four or five of them. And they'd laugh all the way through it."

The woman covered her eyes and lowered her head.

Katie stopped writing and reached out and touched her shoulder. Furiously, she turned toward Ernie and me. "See what your fellow GIs did? These women had to organize themselves and take the law into their own hands."

"Hey," Ernie said, "I just got here."

Outside, something popped—louder than a firecracker—and a whistling round tore through the canvas of the GP tent.

"Do you see anything?"

"No. Do you?"

"Nada."

We had leapt to the floor as soon as the round flew by. Corporal Hurley lay next to us, all three of our heads poking beneath the side canvas of the tent, searching the night.

"They've been doing this every hour or two," she told us, "just to keep us off-balance."

"Who's *they*?" I asked.

"Skinner, Staff Sergeant. And all his boys."

"Wait a minute. Some staff sergeant, a fellow member of your unit, is firing rounds at you and the other female soldiers here? Popping them off whenever he feels like it?"

"Actually, he's in the combat engineer unit. The Four-fifty-fifth. We're just attached to them, temporarily. Transportation support."

"You drive the big trucks that haul the pontoons."

"And maintain those trucks."

The 455th Combat Engineers was a river-crossing unit. Mobile. So they could get to wherever they were tactically required to transport men and equipment across water barriers, rivers or lakes. It was a tough job. And dangerous.

"What about the commanding officer? What about the first sergeant? Don't they have anything to say about this?"

She shrugged. "The first sergeant is back at base camp. Skinner is the NCO in charge of operations, so out here in the field he runs the show."

"And the CO?"

"I'll take you to him," she said.

We slid backward into the tent and then, keeping a low profile, the three of us crouched through the front flap and made our way around to the back of the tent to a cement-block building that by the stench was obviously the latrine.

"The ROK Army built it," she said. "They use this area for training, just like we do."

"Some training," I said.

A man squatted on the ground with his back against the latrine wall, his hands shackled behind him. Another female soldier stood nearby, guarding him, and after receiving a greeting from Corporal Hurley, she switched on a flashlight and held it pointed toward the ground. Moonlight glinted off the man's haggard face. Captain's bars were pinned to his shoulder. I crouched in front of him and identified myself.

"Your name, sir?"

"Captain Angstrom. I'm the CO of Headquarters Company of the Four-fifty-fifth Combat Engineer Battalion."

I showed him my badge. He stared me right in the eye.

"I'm ordering you to untie me and arrest all these women who've illegally taken me into custody."

Hurley fondled the hilt of her .45.

"Let me ask a few questions first, sir," I said.

"No questions, goddamn it. Untie me and get me the hell out of here!"

No matter how I tried to open a dialogue with him, Angstrom refused to engage. Indignant, he just kept ordering us to release him.

"Not much I can do about it," I told him. "They have our weapons."

"Well, get somebody out here who *can* do something about it."

With that outburst, the female guard clicked off the flashlight. Captain Angstrom grunted, moaned, and then hung his head, remaining silent.

Back in the GP tent, Katie Byrd sat on the cot opposite Ernie and me and read us some passages from her notebook.

"Attempted rape," she said. "Routinely. Some of them successful. Ever since they arrived here last week to unload those pontoons. Finally, the women of the transportation unit, fourteen against almost fifty all-male combat engineers, organized themselves under Corporal Hurley's command and started fighting back."

"Who was doing this to them?" Ernie asked.

"Skinner and his little crew, mostly. About a dozen guys. They follow him blindly, like he's a cult leader. The other GIs kept quiet and pretended not to notice what was going on, probably because they were afraid of Skinner and his boys. The CO, Captian Angstrom, they tell me, is a mama's boy who mostly stays inside his command tent, hoping people won't bring problems to him."

"Huh," Ernie said, chuffing out a sound almost resembling a laugh. "Ignorance. The best way to stay out of trouble."

"How about the chain of command?" I asked.

"The battalion commander, Captain Angstrom's boss, the ladies tell me, is a raging misogynist."

"A what?" Ernie asked.

"A sexist. Hates women. Pissed off that they were sent to his unit, even temporarily. Says the army was way more efficient—and peaceful—when there were only men. Until the big change came down from on high a couple of years ago and women began to be assigned to regular army units—they were shuffled off to medical and clerical jobs almost exclusively."

"Just like in 'Nam," Ernie said.

Katie studied him. "What do you mean?"

"You were there," Ernie replied, "as a reporter. You must've seen it. We'd go out on missions to the countryside. The local women knew better than to come anywhere near us. If they did, and the honchos made the mistake of not keeping us busy, any girl we caught would be dragged out into the jungle and forced to do her duty for god and country."

"*Your* god. Your country."

"I guess."

"Did you do that?" Katie asked. "Rape women in Vietnam?"

"Hey, I drove a deuce-and-a-half. With a load of C rations in the back, or worse, crates of high-explosive ammunition. There was no safe place to park the truck where the cargo wouldn't be ripped off."

"So you *didn't* rape women?"

"No need. When we got back to base camp, they were waiting for us at the gate. Plenty of volunteers."

Ernie suddenly realized that Katie was taking notes.

"Hey! You're not going to include that in one of your articles, are you?"

"Why not? You'll be famous."

"That's not the kind of fame I need."

"Too late. You already said it."

He reached for her notebook, but she snatched it away from him. "Keep your hands to yourself." She turned to me. "How about you, Sueño? You ever raped someone?"

"What? Never."

"Would you, if you had the chance?"

"Never," I repeated.

Ernie jabbed his thumb in my direction. "He's a Boy Scout."

"Woodcraft Ranger," I corrected.

"Yeah, that's right. Woodchuck Ranger."

Katie Byrd flipped through the pages. "All right, you two. Anyway, the women of C Company organized themselves. Vigilante protection, you might call it. But still, they were like a herd of wildebeest being preyed upon by hyenas. Eventually one of them got caught."

"Who?"

Katie underlined a name. "Helen Ochs. Private First Class. Hometown: Edina, Minnesota. It was Skinner who ordered her to carry a can of diesel to pontoon number six, beached at the edge of the river."

In the darkness, Ernie and I hadn't even seen the river yet. But we could hear it rushing by.

"Apparently, it was a setup," Katie said. "Ochs never made it. Some of Skinner's boys were waiting near the banks, and when she approached, they dragged her into the bushes, ripped off her fatigue pants, and held her there, muffling her screams until Staff Sergeant Skinner arrived. He did it first, and then his assistant demons took their turns."

Katie was trying to act like the tough journalist she was, but tiny beads of moisture had seeped to the edges of her eyes. She stopped talking.

"So did they turn Skinner in?" I asked.

"Yes. The next day, with Hurley's help and some of the other gals, they approached the CO and told him the whole story. This was less than a week ago. He listened, but didn't call in his company clerk to take notes. Then he told them that he was taking the accusations very seriously but needed to investigate before he went up the chain of command to battalion. And he did. Hurley claims she saw Skinner enter the command tent, followed by a few of the other guys, one by one. Later that day, she and PFC Ochs were called into the CP tent to talk to Captian Angstrom. He told them he'd completed his investigation, and that this was strictly a he-said-she-said situation, as he put it. There was no way he could prefer charges unless they produced some hard evidence.

"With Hurley's coaxing, Private Ochs showed him some of the bruises on her body. But they didn't exactly have any scientific way to prove she'd been raped. The only medic assigned to this operation is some sleepy-headed guy who can barely manage to hand out bicarbonate of soda."

"Captain Angstrom didn't notify battalion or call in law enforcement?"

Katie shook her head. "Neither. Early the next morning, before dawn, Ochs disappeared. When Corporal Hurley and some of the other gals went searching for her, they found her wool cap and field jacket on the rotting wooden boards at the end of the pier. Apparently, she threw herself into the river."

Both Ernie and I were silent.

"She left a note," Katie added.

She handed it to me. It basically explained the same story Katie had just told us and asked that any of her personal effects back at Camp Long be forwarded to her mother. She left the address, which was the Rolling Hills Mobile Home Park in Edina, Minnesota. Space 14A.

I showed the note to Ernie, who read it, and when he was finished he handed it back to Katie Byrd.

"Did they find the body?" I asked.

"They haven't even looked," Katie said. "Angstrom won't allow it; says they don't have time. More than a few ROK Army units have had to be ferried across the river in the last few days."

"Did they show him the note?"

"He waved it off. Said he wasn't interested in 'hysterical ranting' as he called it."

"He doesn't want a rape allegation or a suicide allegation on his record," Ernie told her. "His chances of being promoted to major would evaporate."

"Why?"

"They would say he had crime in his unit because of piss-poor leadership. Safer for battalion to promote a company commander who doesn't have a record involving crime."

"Thus giving every military officer a motive to cover for criminals."

"Welcome to Eighth Army bureaucracy," Ernie said. "And it's worse than that. In this post-Vietnam army, it's up or out. An officer either keeps getting promoted, or he's passed over and eventually forced out of the service. And no matter how many years he's invested or how dependent his family is on his military income, he'll be unable to finish his twenty years and qualify for a monthly pension, medical care, or any of the other bennies the army offers."

"So they *can't* report rape," Katie said.

"Most of them see it that way," I said.

Katie shook her head. "Fucked-up system. All Angstrom has done so far is report Private Ochs as missing, presumed absent without leave. Apparently, the battalion commander is accepting that explanation for now because, in his opinion, women can't handle the rigors of long field deployments. He figures she'll show up in some hotel in Wonju and eventually turn herself in."

"But Hurley knows better."

"Everyone knows better," Katie said.

"So Hurley and the others finally had enough," Ernie said. "They banded together and took up arms."

"Yes. Four days ago. The first thing they did was take the CO into custody. That's when they contacted me, and apparently one of them drove down to Wonju and express-delivered a photo of themselves to me at the Bando."

"And you forwarded it to Hong Kong and ran it in the Sunday edition of the *Overseas Observer*."

"Timing is everything in print journalism."

"They gave up on using the chain of command."

"Too many women have been assaulted, and not a damn thing has been done about it. For them, PFC Helen Ochs was the last straw."

"What do they expect to happen?" I asked. "What good can come of something like this? It's mutiny."

"They don't know the consequences, and, frankly, they don't give a damn. They just want the whole story to come out. That's why I'm here."

Another round exploded through the side of the tent. The three of us fell to the ground. While down there, Ernie said, "Maybe I ought to arrest the sonofabitch who keeps shooting at us."

"Maybe you should," Katie agreed.

■　■　■

Ernie insisted that he go and I stay behind.

"I need a rescue squad standing by in case they don't trust me and decide to lock me up or worse. Besides, you look too much like a Boy Scout, Sueño. Or a Woodchuck Ranger."

"Woodcraft Ranger," I corrected again.

"Whatever. I'll make my way to their bivouac area," he told me. "I'll show them my badge and tell them that I'm from the Criminal Investigation Division and that there's been a report of a disturbance here in the Four-fifty-fifth. You can bet they'll want to lay all the blame on Corporal Hurley and her girls."

"How about PFC Ochs? You going to ask about her?"

"Only if they bring it up, which they probably won't." Ernie thought about it for a moment. "I'll need my .45 back, and I'm not sure how long this is going to take. I have to win Staff Sergeant Skinner's confidence somehow, then isolate him, take him into custody, and bring him back here."

"That's when you'll need me," I said.

"Yeah, probably. And maybe some extra firepower from Hurley and the girls."

"Maybe we should go back to Camp Long," I said. "Try to reason with the battalion commander. Get him to take action."

"Too late for that," Ernie said. "If the brass wanted to do something about this situation, they would've done it by now. Especially since Katie Byrd has informed the Chief of Staff about it, and he still hasn't lifted a finger."

"He might be planning something."

"He might, but we can't assume that. Skinner's dangerous. He has to be stopped now."

"I'm looking forward to interrogating him. If we can get him to admit to even part of what he's done, that'll go a long way in making it more difficult for Eighth Army to cover this up."

"Okay," Ernie said. "I'm going in."

I saw the wisdom of that and nodded.

"We need a signal," I said.

Ernie thought about it, then told me what it would be.

"What are you going to tell them?"

He shrugged. "I'll play it by ear. About the only thing we can count on is that they're going to want to tell me how innocent they are and how rotten the women are."

"Maybe they are innocent," I said. "We're impartial enforcers of the law. We have to keep an open mind."

Ernie must've sensed the lack of conviction in my voice. He snorted a laugh. "I know GIs. Especially when they're in the field." He waved his arm to indicate the isolation of the Taebaek Mountains. "Out here at night, with no one watching, there's no telling how far a group of them will go."

"Even as far as murder?" I said.

"Easy. Any one of those rounds they've been firing could've killed someone. Which is why I have to go in before this shit gets any further out of hand."

Ernie headed downhill toward the river and the main

bivouac area, about a hundred yards away. After less than a minute, I heard someone faintly yell "Halt!" and then an answering voice. Ernie's. After that, mumbling and then silence, once again.

No gunshots, which I took to be a good sign.

The next morning, I leaned against a boulder on the edge of a cliff overlooking the river, sipping on a canteen cup full of hot coffee. The signal we had set up was Ernie firing three times into the air with his .45 or, if that wasn't possible, a clanging of metal in the Morse code I had taught him for SOS. Three dots, three dashes, and three dots again. I just hoped that, in the excitement, he didn't forget the pattern. But as on edge as I was, any repeated metal clanging would probably lead me to go down there. Every time I heard a mess kit knock against one of the huge army-issue serving pans, I sat up, startled.

Corporal Hurley and two of her best female soldiers were nearby and on alert to accompany me downhill to the bivouac area if needed.

Katie Byrd Worthington walked up and squatted next to me. "Maybe they'll boil him in one of those enormous pots," she said.

"Huh?"

"You know, like those old movies where the missionary is captured and the natives start cooking him in a big iron pot."

"To eat him, you mean?"

"Yeah. Maybe they're low on protein. And I don't put anything past these cretins."

I looked away to study the encampment. "You don't have a very high opinion of GIs."

"*Au contraire*. I actually do. But some of them are rotten to the core. The festering pus of an infection."

"Lovely way to put it."

"Hey, I'm a wordsmith, remember?"

"Nobody reads your articles."

Katie started and turned to stare at me more directly. "Maybe you're right," she said, "but they sure as hell ogle the photographs. And study the headlines. Sometimes they even read the photo captions."

"Yeah. *Vivian from Paris suns herself on a sandy beach.*"

"Hey, the *Overseas Observer* isn't all cheesecake."

"You're right. The GIs also pay close attention to the car advertisements. After all the walking we do here in Frozen Chosun, the yearning to own a car can lead to overpriced loans with impossible repayment terms. But mostly, the GIs study the girls in the bikinis."

"Okay, okay. So I don't write for the *New Yorker*."

I turned to her. "Is that it? The *New Yorker*? Is that the magazine people see as having the most prestige?"

She shrugged. "It's up there. There's a lot of other good ones too, but I'd say the *New Yorker* is at the top of most people's list." She studied me. "How far did you get in school?"

"I dropped out in my senior year of high school. Joined the army."

"But you like to learn things, don't you? Like the Korean language, the culture, the motivations driving a society so different from ours." When I didn't answer, she said, "You don't have to be bashful with me, Sueño. I'm not like the guys in the barracks. I won't make fun of you for wanting to be something better."

I grinned. "And what do you know about the barracks? A nice lady like you."

"Whoa, a *lady*? Haven't been called that in a while."

I laughed. "Not by the Eighth Army officer corps, that's for sure."

"What *do* they call me?"

I started to open my mouth, but she said, "Never mind. Don't answer that."

We sat in silence for a while before she asked, "Do you think Bascom will be able to pull this off?"

"If anybody can."

"You have a lot of confidence in him, don't you?" Then she added, "Actually, you both have a lot of confidence in each other."

"I guess we do."

"I'll try not to get you in too much trouble when I write this article," she said, "if that's what you're worried about."

"I'm not worried about that."

"Why not?"

"They'll blame us no matter what happens. Whatever's good, they take credit for. Whatever's bad, they blame on the enlisted men."

"You whining?"

"No. Just being realistic. It's the way of the world."

What was maybe a large spoon started banging on what was maybe a large pot. Three quick, then three slow and three fast.

"That's him," I said, rising to my feet.

"They plopped him into the stew that fast?"

"Chef's special," I said and ran toward the GP tent.

We decided to loop around the bivouac area until we reached the river, which I'd come to learn was the Pyeongchang River. At the shore, we regrouped behind a dune topped with weeds. Hurley and I conferred on the best way to approach Sergeant Skinner and his minions. She and one of the two female soldiers would proceed on the right flank and take a position behind the clump of tents. Me and a certain Private Muñoz, with one of the M16 automatic rifles, would make our way along the riverbank to where the row of pontoons sat beached along the shore. From there we'd make a pincer movement back to meet up, hopefully at about where the Morse code clanging seemed to have come from.

"What do we do when we find him?" Hurley asked.

"Ernie will brief you on what he needs done. If we don't find him, we still want Staff Sergeant Skinner. The fact that he's the ranking man and he allowed someone to take potshots at us all night is enough to make the arrest. You all recognize him, right?"

They nodded their assent.

"If you can, isolate him and force him up to the bluff where we can hold him at the Command Post."

"What do we do with him then?" one of the women asked, flexing her trigger finger.

"We'll decide that later. Any questions?"

"Nope. Get Skinner first. Agent Ernie if we can."

"That's it. Good luck."

They nodded, but before they left, I said, "One more thing. I know how you must feel, but now's not the time to take out your anger on Skinner or any of the other men in this outfit, no matter how deserving they are. With any luck, Ernie has already neutralized our target and all you'll have to do is escort them to the top of the bluff. This is law enforcement. You can't let emotions get the better of you."

The three women grew quiet. Hurley stared at me. Finally, she said, "You have no idea how we feel."

I didn't respond.

Without further comment, she and her backup took off toward the tents.

Private Muñoz and I crept along the waterline toward the pontoons, keeping as close to the river's edge as we could so the rise toward the high banks would keep us hidden. When we reached the pontoons, we crouched behind ancient wooden timbers that served as a stanchion for the pier and studied the encampment. Quiet. Very little activity, except for someone puttering around the big square two-and-a-half-ton mess truck. Not very disciplined, I thought. No morning formation, no roll call, no buzz of activity as the night guard was relieved and new sentries took over. Discipline was definitely slipping here. And then I figured out why.

I nudged Private Muñoz. "That old Korean man over there, next to the cart. Have you seen him before?"

"Yeah. He showed up when we first arrived, selling ramen and soju and Fanta. Captain Angstrom chased him away."

"He's back."

"I'll say."

The old man was slipping empty bottles of the orange soft drink into the wooden case they came in and, once the case was full, shoving it back inside the open hold of his pushcart. He was also placing the smaller, 375-milliliter empty bottles of soju, the fierce Korean rice liquor, into their stenciled twelve-pack boxes. As we watched, he traipsed between the tents, picking up bottles that had been haphazardly tossed into the mud, draining those that still had a smidgen of liquid left in them, and then sliding them back into their slots in their wooden crates.

"Looks like business is good," I said.

"Which is why everybody's sleeping so late," she said. "They got wasted last night."

We were almost an hour past dawn, late by army standards.

"Now all we gotta do is find Ernie," I said.

"And Skinner," she added, withering disdain in her voice.

I almost asked if she'd had a run-in with Skinner but figured that just asking the question might be insulting. Best to keep focused on the current mission.

"Do you know which tent Skinner might be in?"

"No," she answered. "Since we took Captain Angstrom, they've moved everything around."

"Why?"

"Probably because Mule wants his boys close to him."

"Mule?"

"What we call Skinner. That and Donkey Dick." She looked at me, flushing slightly. "Because it's disgusting, not big."

I didn't ask how she knew.

Moving the tents around made sense. Military rank hierarchy no longer ruled in this unit. Now it was all about who was most loyal to Mule Skinner. He'd want his most dedicated henchmen nearby.

The old Korean man slowly rolled his cart uphill, picking up empties as he went.

"Where's he going?" I asked.

"Probably to the far side of the ridgeline. There's a village over there, and I suppose that's where he gets his soju and Fanta."

Orange soda and rice liquor combined. While in the field,

the American GI's favorite cocktail. It might not taste like much, but it got the job done.

Someone poked their head out the front flap of one of the tents.

"There he is," I said.

Ernie.

At first, he looked back and forth but didn't see us. I leaned away from the ancient wooden stanchion and waved my right hand. He saw me and waved back, signaling frantically for us to come fast.

"Let's go."

We hurried forward in a crouch, Muñoz right behind me, keeping her M16 rifle at the ready. When I got close, Ernie hissed. "Don't let that cart go. Make him bring it back." I immediately understood what he had in mind.

So did Muñoz. "I'll do it," she said and took off up the hill after him.

Ernie waved me in, and I crouched through the flap into the darkness. The interior was lit by only a dim field lamp. Next to it was a fold-down wooden table, a couple of metal chairs, and a cot containing a tall man still wearing his fatigues with his combat boots hanging off the bottom edge. He was thin, with a narrow black mustache and dark hair that wanted to curl but couldn't because it was cropped too short. His snoring sounded like an Alaskan sawmill.

"How much did he drink last night?" I asked.

"All I could coax into him. Since I was buying, that was a lot."

"You became buddies?"

"Famous friends. He was convinced that I was going to arrest all the 'bitches,' as he called them, for kidnapping Angstrom. And he even started to believe that he'd get a medal for holding the unit together."

"Holding his band of rapists and bullies together is more like it."

Ernie nodded.

"What about the other guys?" I asked.

"Most of them are about as drunk as their boss. Now's the time to get this son of a bitch out of here."

And as I surmised, the open interior of a Korean wooden pushcart would be the perfect place to stow him.

Muñoz peeked through the flap. "Got the cart," she said. "He says he's going to want some money though."

"Tell him we'll take care of him. Make room inside. Get those cases of empty bottles out of there."

"Right," she said and disappeared.

Ernie and I approached Skinner and looked down at him. He still snored heavily. "You take the legs," Ernie said. "I'll grab him by the armpits."

As we struggled to lift him, Ernie said, "He stinks."

"No showers out here," I said.

"There's a freaking river."

We managed to lift him, and by dragging him and bumping his butt along the ground, we reached the front flap and were just about to push through when stinky Staff Sergeant Mule Skinner came alive. An eyelid popped open, awareness filled the eyeball behind it, and then he kicked me in the stomach in a way that befitted his nickname.

I dropped his legs, floundered backward, and tumbled off-balance into the mud. As I tried to raise myself, Ernie was shoving Sergeant Skinner, who had twisted and somehow managed to get both feet below him and was cursing now and throwing punches. Ernie popped a straight left jab at his jaw, but it wasn't enough to slow him down. A vicious windmill of fury and fists erupted from Mule Skinner, along with spittle and invective. The blows rained down on Ernie's head and shoulders like a stormfront moving toward Indianapolis.

I clambered back to my feet. Skinner was so intent on beating the crap out of Ernie that he didn't hear me coming. I landed a short right uppercut into his kidney. It had the desired effect. His back straightened, arched like a flexed bow, and as he turned, I slammed him with a left to the jaw, then a right to the stomach. He went down.

As Staff Sergeant Skinner lay in a heap on the ground, Ernie said, "That oughta hold him for a while."

We dragged him outside to the cart and stuffed him into the now-empty hold, tucking his hands and his combat boots in last. The old Korean man, the owner of the cart, stood watching us, mouth agape.

"*Kapshida*," I told him. Let's go. I started pushing the cart.

The old man followed, shaking his head in amazement. Was there no end to the shenanigans American GIs could come up with?

We were halfway up the ridge when the first shot rang out.

Ernie pulled his .45 and I pulled mine, and Private Muñoz knelt and aimed her rifle toward the center of the encampment. At first we didn't see anyone, but then about a half-dozen guys, all with M16 rifles aimed right at us, stepped out from behind the tents.

"Drop it," one of them growled.

We could fire, probably hurt, or even kill, one or more of them. But when they opened fire on us, we would last about three seconds before being totally shredded by a jillion automatic rounds. It didn't seem like the smart thing to do.

Still, I hesitated. Given their record, who knew what these guys would do to Private Muñoz? Or Ernie and me, for that matter? And now, with them knowing the 8th Army Criminal Investigation Division was on their case, would they attack the women at the Command Post? Go berserk and start shooting everyone there? Maybe not, but how could I be sure?

Once again, the guy growled ominously. "I said *drop it*."

Ernie clanged the slide back on his .45. "Take a flying leap, asshole."

Somebody, I thought—on their side or ours—was going to be the first to pull a trigger. Should it be me? Just as the survival calculation raced through my brain, a bright light expanded like a nova atop one of the pontoons on the river. Almost simultaneously, the sonic blast of the explosion hit us, and debris started zinging through the air like a hive of maddened hornets.

Everybody crouched.

And then they went off, one after another, like a row of firecrackers. One pontoon, the next, and then the next until all six were nothing but smoldering ruins.

The old man hurried forward, opened the side of his cart, and began frantically tugging on Sergeant Skinner's leg. Awake now, Skinner managed, through a series of contortions, to emerge from the cart after bumping his head a couple of times. He stood up and groggily stared down on the remnants of what had once been river-crossing pontoons.

"What the fuck?" he said.

"Commandos," I told him, remembering the classified document Strange had misappropriated. It must have told the NKs exactly where and how the river-crossing operation would be conducted. "Precision raid," I continued. "They knew where to find you."

"Christ," Ernie said.

And who knew what other mischief the North Koreans were up to throughout the vast Focus Lens operational area.

"Take defensive positions," I told the men around us. "They might be coming after us next."

Forgetting personal differences, the men scattered. Ernie and Private Muñoz and I climbed quickly to the top of the ridge. The old man grabbed his cart, shoved it forward, and started running as fast as he could away from the GI bivouac.

Atop the ridge, just ten yards from the temporary headquarters set up by Corporal Hurley and her adherents, Katie Byrd lay prone behind a row of sandbags. Camera out, she twisted the lens settings and zeroed in on the burnt husks of the exploded pontoons.

"What the hell happened?" she asked, without looking up, as we approached.

"Sappers," Ernie replied.

"What?" Katie asked.

"Commandos with bombs," Ernie explained.

"But who—"

"North Koreans," Ernie said. "Who else?" He grabbed Katie and tried to pull her to her feet. She twisted her arm and shrugged him off.

"We need to get out of here," Ernie said. "Now!"

In the distance, automatic fire laced the shoreline.

"They're fighting back," I said.

Ernie squinted and studied the scene. "All the fire's one way," he said, "toward the river. A waste of time. Now that they've set off their charges, you can expect those commandos to disappear. They have plenty of other targets to get to. A few half-drunk GIs aren't of particular interest to them."

By now, Corporal Hurley had joined us. I turned to her. "You have to release Captain Angstrom," I said.

She looked at some of the other female soldiers who'd gathered around us, all of them holding their rifles expectantly. "Why should we?" she asked. "We were being raped and brutalized, and he did *nothing*. All he can do is keep repeating his he-said-she-said bullshit. As far as I'm concerned, we ought to turn him over to the North Koreans, for all the good he's done us."

A few murmurs of assent passed through the crowd, but more faces turned away.

"We'll get to that," Ernie said in a voice that, for him, was surprisingly reasonable. "My partner and I have witnessed what's gone down here. A report will be made, an official one that can't be ignored, about this unit and the death of Private Helen Ochs."

"They'll bury it," Hurley insisted, shaking her head.

Katie Byrd finished fiddling with her camera and stuck it into the canvas holder. "They might *try* to bury it," she said, "but I'll keep it alive. Me and the *Overseas Observer*. After my story comes out, you can all send a copy of the article to your congressmen back home. And your hometown newspaper. The army hates bad publicity more than Dracula hates sunburn." She jabbed her thumb toward Ernie and me. "I've worked with these guys before. They might not be much to look at, but they don't give up. Neither do I."

"So why should we do Angstrom a favor?" one of the women asked.

"You'll be doing yourself a favor," I told her. "Eighth Army will want to keep this entire incident as low-key as possible. Arresting and detaining a commanding officer is a serious charge, but they'll avoid bringing it if they can. Letting the situation deteriorate as far as it did reflects poorly on their own leadership. If you let Angstrom go now, he might not even mention it when he's debriefed. It's too humiliating. And even if the honchos find out about it, they'll do their best to ignore it. But if you keep him shackled too long, there might be no choice but for Eighth Army to bring you all up on charges for false imprisonment of a superior officer."

"Are you a freaking lawyer?"

"No. But I know how their minds work. The honchos will try to minimize all charges, if possible. They don't want the bad publicity of an armed female mutiny. Here, in Eighth Army, they don't want it, and the Pentagon sure as hell doesn't want it. How would it look to their recruiting effort? Without the draft, the army needs new recruits, both men and women. This could set back their numbers for years."

Another round of automatic fire erupted below. I studied the river.

"Driftwood," Ernie said. "Skinner and his boys are getting paranoid. Firing at logs in the river."

"You sure the commandos are gone?"

"They were probably halfway to their next target before those charges even went off."

I thought about me and Muñoz crouching just next to the first pontoon before the explosions started, wondering if a North Korean had us in his sights, but forced the thought out of my mind.

Hurley acquiesced. She turned to me and said, "I'll release Captain Angstrom. Based on your promise that Eighth Army won't be able to cover this up." She shook her forefinger at me. "You can't let us down."

"We won't," I said.

"But we won't disband. We'll keep our weapons, we'll keep our own GP tent, and we'll keep a rotation on guard duty to make sure those creeps don't bother us." She pointed downhill toward Skinner and his boys. "Angstrom can join them, but he better not mess with *us*." She jabbed her thumb into the center of her chest.

The other women nodded and murmured their assent. As a group, they walked back toward the cement-walled latrine and unshackled Captain Angstrom. He collected himself quickly—straightened his uniform, rubbed his face in handfuls of cold water, and combed his hair.

His first act was to radio battalion headquarters and report the demolition of the six pontoons. He was ordered to salvage what he could and return to Camp Long with all his men and equipment as soon as possible. While talking to the battalion operations officer, he didn't mention rape accusations or his incarceration or the insurrection his unit had just experienced. And my guess was that he wouldn't. He was already in a hell of a lot of hot water. A missing female soldier—namely, Private Helen Ochs—would be difficult to explain, though not as difficult as a mutiny.

Once he had signed off with battalion, he glanced at the women warily, and then, without a further word, returned to the main bivouac area. From a distance, it didn't look as if Skinner was happy to see him, since he was no longer the top dog. They launched a mop-up operation but were unable to find any enemy soldiers. Ernie had been right. The commandos had long since disappeared.

"Are we at war?" Katie asked.

"I don't know," I replied. "It's probably just a harassment operation to disrupt the joint military exercise. The North Koreans have done it before. They hate Focus Lens."

"Why?"

"Because it keeps our American and South Korean units sharp. Ready to defend against what the Great Leader wants more than anything, another all-out invasion in order to unite the Korean people under his glorious banner."

"If we were at war," Ernie said, "we'd be hearing more

explosions in the distance. And more combat aircraft flying overhead."

"But that doesn't mean the North Koreans won't miscalculate and go too far," Katie Byrd said.

"Or one of our units will miscalculate," Ernie replied. "And maybe lob a few artillery shells behind North Korean lines."

"Isn't that sort of thing controlled by central command?"

"Theoretically, yes. But boys will be boys."

Katie shook her head. "Kids playing with matches."

"While dancing atop a keg of gunpowder," I added.

-12-

Now that it was daylight, Ernie made good time through the mountains. Once we reached Wonju, we didn't bother to stop at Camp Long. Katie wasn't the only one anxious to return to Seoul. For her it was to file a hot story. For us, it was a different reason. After Katie dozed off in the back seat, Ernie turned to me and said, "I know what you're thinking."

"Yeah, what?"

"Strange. And the document about the Focus Lens deployments. That's how the North Koreans knew where to find the river-crossing pontoons."

"Maybe."

The North Koreans didn't have an airborne reconnaissance capability. We'd shoot down their planes too easily. The US and South Korean airforces ruled the skies. So with no overhead surveillance, no way to keep an eye on what our military units were doing, they had to rely on other, more traditional ways of gathering intelligence. Like targeting a lonely GI with access to classified information and using a beautiful woman to persuade him to share.

"There'll probably be more attacks," Ernie added.

"Yeah, but our side's on alert now."

"Still, if the NKs know when and where our units are going to deploy, they could set up some pretty effective ambushes."

I nodded. He had a helluva point.

Ernie stepped on the gas.

I worried what North Korea's next move would be. Who would get hurt? And whose fault would it be? Maybe ours.

The ROK Army military checkpoints were out in full force. The North Korean attack on an American river-crossing unit might not ever be publicized in the newspapers or television—the Park Chung-hee regime wouldn't want to engender panic—but military and law enforcement agencies were well aware of the incident. We reached the first ROK Army barricade near the Gwangjin Bridge just before crossing the Han River. And we were stopped again near Seobinggo as we entered the Yongsan district on the southern edge of Seoul.

"Where the hell are you taking me?" Katie asked.

Ernie shrugged. "Thought you might want to stop at Eighth Army first. Check with the Public Affairs Office, see if there are any updates on North Korean activity."

"Oh no, you don't. You're not trapping me on that compound. I want to go back to the Bando. Now!"

"I thought you checked out of there," Ernie said.

"I did," she replied, "for about five minutes. I was sitting in the coffee shop, and I saw the military vehicles pull up with the MPs, so I told the front desk that I was checking out with no forwarding address. Then I returned to the coffee shop and hid behind the coffee urn."

"So the front desk lied to them."

"No," Katie Byrd replied, slightly offended. "I'd officially checked out."

"But you reregistered as soon as the MPs left."

"No crime in that."

"Bet the front desk wouldn't lie to the Korean Army," I said, "if they came knocking."

"Humph!" Katie said, crossing her arms. "Not my problem if they're afraid of their own army."

When Ernie hesitated before making the turn downtown, Katie said, "Don't make me tell Frankie Baby that you guys aren't escorting me the way he ordered. If I don't file this story on the river-crossing unit"—she slapped her notebook—"then we'll have to run a filler. Like photos of a certain brigadier general performing a certain nude dance with a lady of questionable virtue."

"All right, already," Ernie said. "The Bando it is."

Ernie swerved toward Namsan Tunnel Number 3 and somehow resisted honking as we rolled through it. When we emerged we made our way through the swirling downtown

Seoul traffic toward the centrally located Bando. Eventually Ernie pulled under the covered entranceway where a liveried doorman helped Katie out of the jeep. She whispered something to him, and immediately he waved his gloved hand and whistled for a kimchi cab. Like magic, the cab appeared, and Katie climbed in and sped off.

"Where in the hell is she going?" Ernie asked.

"To file her story, like she did before. And ship her most recent set of photographs to Hong Kong."

"Rude."

"Why do you say that?"

"She didn't even say goodbye. Or thank us for the ride."

"That's her," I said.

"Are all reporters like that?"

"I wouldn't know."

It dawned on me that I knew very little about practicing professionals in any field outside of the military, a thought that slightly depressed me. But I knew about the ones I needed to know about, including detectives for the Korean National Police.

"Where to?" Ernie asked, shoving his red devil gearshift forward.

"Mr. Kill," I said.

Ernie glanced at me, exasperated. "Aren't we ever gonna take a break?"

"No rest for the wicked," I said.

Especially when North Korean commandos were ravaging the countryside based on confidential information they had possibly received from our good old buddy of the hot chocolate with two marshmallows: the man called Strange.

Chief Homicide Inspector Gil Kwon-up motioned for us to take a seat on an upholstered bench on the far side of a varnished coffee table. He sat in a chair opposite us.

"Finally," he said. "You're here. I've been waiting."

"We've been sort of preoccupied," I said.

"So I understand. Something about an incident near the Pyeongchang River."

The Korean National Police were the only police force in the country; local jurisdictions weren't allowed to have police forces. The central government didn't want any competition. As such, the KNPs had police stations in virtually every city, town, and hamlet in the Republic of Korea, from the DMZ to the Port of Pusan. In addition, they had operatives, official and unofficial, gathering information twenty-four seven. Still, I was constantly amazed at how quickly and efficiently the KNPs relayed intelligence.

"You might say we're still recovering from that." I rubbed my chin.

He examined us. Our two-day-old stubble, the unkempt clothing, and effusive body odor. Koreans sometimes said that

Americans smelled like meat. Today, I imagined, we smelled more like sweat and mud and fear.

"Congratulations on your diligence," he said. "Unfortunately, I have a new job for you two."

"Something good?" Ernie asked.

"Something excellent," Mr. Kill added. "So much so you might not survive the assignment." Kill turned toward his personal assistant, Officer Oh. Looking sharp in her KNP duty uniform—navy-blue skirt and powder-blue blouse—she'd been standing unobtrusively near the door. He murmured something to her in Korean, and she bowed, turned, and stepped out of the room.

"What is it?" Ernie asked.

"You'll see," Mr.Kill replied.

We sat quietly for one minute, maybe two. Then Officer Oh returned, holding open the door.

"Someone you know, I believe," Mr. Kill said.

Looking haggard and disheveled in an unpressed khaki uniform, a man walked in. We knew him, and we knew him well. Sergeant First Class Harvey.

Without being prompted, he sat down in an empty chair. "Collapsed" is probably the most precise term. Utterly exhausted. He slipped off his shades, rubbed his eyes for a moment, and put the sunglasses back on. Staring at us gamely, he waggled his empty cigarette holder between thin lips.

"Had any *strange* lately?" he asked.

-13-

"What the hell happened to you?" Ernie asked.

"They pulled me out of the field exercise," Strange answered, "ordered me back to Seoul. Then Mr. Kill here gave me a secret mission. Very dangerous, very hush-hush."

"*You?* Hush-hush? Doing what?"

"I told you. It's a secret."

Mr. Kill interrupted. "We've asked him to help us find Kim Yoon-jeong. The woman who Sergeant Harvey here entrusted with the classified document concerning unit deployments during Focus Lens."

"The North Korean woman," Ernie said.

"Exactly."

Ernie turned back to Strange. "Have you found her?"

Strange squirmed in his seat. "Not exactly."

"Well, what *exactly* did happen, then?"

Strange looked over at Mr. Kill. Mr. Kill spoke."He got lost."

"Got lost? Here in Seoul?"

Strange nodded.

"Because you can't read the signs? Or because you couldn't find your thumb if it was stuck halfway up your ass?"

I reached over and patted Ernie's forearm. "Take it easy."

"Oh, I'll take it easy all right," Ernie continued. "Yesterday, probably because of information *you* passed on to the North Koreans, six pricey pontoon barges were blasted into smithereens." He pointed at Strange.

Strange's back straightened and his thin lips pursed. "You mishandled the same document," he said.

"We gave it to a GI who was authorized to handle it. You gave it to your freaking girlfriend."

"She's not my girlfriend."

"Well, that's for sure. We all know you couldn't get an *actual* girlfriend if you tried."

Mr. Kill held up both his hands. He glanced toward Officer Oh and with his eyes motioned for her to leave the room. She did, closing the door behind her.

"We have important work to do, gentlemen. The squabbling can wait until later."

Mr. Kill's English never ceased to amaze me; the fact that he could so easily slip in a word like "squabble." His university education here in Korea, along with graduate work in the States, had definitely paid off. That coupled with the fact that he had served as a detective in one of the toughest police forces in the world for over twenty years made me defer to him on almost every occasion.

After Strange and Ernie quieted down, I said, "So what's our mission?"

"To find Kim Yoon-jeong." He studied the three of us. "And don't worry about your military duties. My superiors have already cleared this with your Chief of Staff. You've been released to work with the Korean National Police until this issue is resolved."

"So they know about the security breach?"

"They do now." Mr. Kill nodded toward Strange. "He told them."

"And they didn't lock you up?" Ernie asked, turning back to Strange.

"They released me to help with this."

"No charges?" I asked.

"Not yet. They said it depends on how well I cooperate."

"Surely," I addressed Mr. Kill, keeping my voice low, "with your resources it would be much easier for you to find her than it would be for the three of us."

"One would think so," he replied. "The difference is that you three have something that the entire Korean National Police Force doesn't have."

"What's that?" I asked.

"Bait," he said, turning his head to Strange.

Strange's eyes widened, and he gulped down what I imagined was a moist wad of phlegm. "Bait?" he asked.

"On a hook," Ernie added. "Pierced and wriggling."

"A staked goat," Ernie said.

"That's our boy," I agreed.

After spending over an hour interrogating Strange about his North Korean friend, we had a much better picture of who she was and how he'd come to meet her. He was bashful about it at first and especially reluctant to reveal the intimate details that Ernie so aggressively probed him for.

Ever the sensitive professional, Ernie asked, "Did you get laid on the first date?"

"None of your damn business," Strange responded.

"Hey, if you couldn't get it up, don't be ashamed. It happens to the best of us, right, Sueño? Not me, of course, but the best of us."

Like a battering ram assaulting a medieval fortress, Ernie gradually broke down Strange's defenses. By the end of the night, Sergeant First Class Cecil B. Harvey was wiping tears from his eyes and explaining the whole thing, from first kiss to heartfelt farewell.

Finally, we left him alone in the interrogation room and stepped out into the hallway.

Ernie said, "Background music would've been nice."

"It worked for Ali MacGraw."

"Who?"

"You know, *Love Story*."

"Must've missed that one."

"Don't worry. You didn't miss much. Other than feeling bummed to see Ray Milland getting old."

"So how the hell are we going to find her?" Ernie asked. "This North Korean woman."

"We take Strange to the old places they used to frequent."

"Besides the *nakji* hideout?"

"There must be more like it."

Ernie thought it over. "Might work, except we can't afford to wait that freaking long. Not with a band of North Korean commandos on the rampage."

"What else can we do?"

"We've got to find a shortcut."

"Like what?"

"Beats the hell out of me."

Mr. Kill's plan made sense. We were to find the North Korean woman, the *nakji* restaurant owner, Mr. Shin—who appeared to be her handler—and bust the entire spy ring wide open. Once they were in custody, the KNPs would take over and use their tried-and-true interrogation techniques, work backward toward the spies' contact with the North Korean military, maybe even feed the commandos false information that would lead them into a trap.

No matter how much mileage they could get out of the

secret document Strange had provided, they knew that the US and South Korean forces would pivot immediately. Now that their war game dispositions had been compromised, unit deployments would be changed. So if the Commies wanted to continue to disrupt Focus Lens—and given Kim Il-sung's single-minded hatred of the joint military exercise, we believed they would—they needed updated information. The logical place to get that information was from the NCO-in-charge of the 8th United States Army classified documents section—namely, our boy Strange.

"I've never been fishing before," Ernie said.

"Me neither."

"Not even when you were a Woodchuck Ranger?"

"Woodcraft Ranger."

"Yeah, that too. You didn't go fishing then?"

"Not even then. I don't think our troop leader knew how." I glanced at Ernie. "How have you never gone fishing? You grew up near Detroit. Don't they call that the Land of a Thousand Lakes?"

"That's Minnesota. And it's ten thousand. But I was too busy to fish."

"Doing what?"

"Serving time in juvie."

"And they drafted you anyway?"

"The draft board didn't know about it. As a minor, my criminal record was sealed."

"Lucky for you."

"Lucky for the army."

That was debatable, but I let it slide.

"Our first decision is where to dangle our bait."

"Itaewon," Ernie said. "They'll expect it."

"I suppose you're right. The other places he ventured out to in Seoul were all with her." Most GIs didn't feel comfortable too far from base, since they didn't speak much Korean and the signs looked like gibberish to them.

"Let's ask Strange where he feels he can most easily find her?"

"Good idea."

We reentered the interrogation room and asked him. His answer surprised us, to put it mildly.

We returned Strange to his quarters on base and reminded him that he was only on probation with the Korean National Police, and if he tried to run, the next time they caught him he'd be locked away, maybe for good. Espionage was a capital offense in the Republic of Korea. Even for a foreigner.

He assured us that he understood he was being given a break and we didn't have to worry. He'd cooperate. That gave us all a chance to catch some rest, but we told him we'd be back to start the night's mission at 2000 hours. Eight P.M.

Ernie and I returned to the barracks. Too tired to eat, I took a luxurious shower, then caught a few hours' sleep. By eight that night, Ernie and I were wearing clean blue jeans and clean sports shirts and were pounding on Strange's door. For a split second I was worried that he'd taken off on us, but the door swung open, and he stared up at us through opaque sunglasses.

"Don't say it," Ernie warned him, "or I'll pop you right in that cigarette holder."

Strange pretended to zip his lips.

The three of us marched to the jeep.

We drove west, through a district known as Mapo, until we finally reached the banks of the Han River. Moonlight illuminated the calm waters from here to the open rice paddies on the far side. As if straight out of an old painting, a single-masted sailboat with a huge wooden rudder sat in the middle of the water, lines dangling off the side, and fishermen doing what they had been doing since time immemorial: catching their daily sustenance with only the aid of the wind and the currents and their God-given intelligence.

As we pulled into the tiny, gravel-covered parking lot, the smell of the restaurant hit us like the slap of a glove. Frying fish. A huge white placard above the entranceway was emblazoned with letters in *hangul*. One word: *nakji*. Next to it, in bright colors, was a giant painted octopus, pink and wriggling, above more Korean lettering that promised the best seafood in the city of Seoul.

"She brought you here?" Ernie asked.

"Many times. And we brought her mom and her three kids, too."

"Nice family outing."

"Yeah." Strange crossed his arms and stared skyward dreamily, savoring the memory.

"What'd you eat?"

"Me?"

"Yeah, you. I know you're grossed out by *nakji*."

"I ate rice," Strange replied. "And a little cabbage kimchi, after I rinsed off the garlic and red pepper paste in those cups of barley tea they always give you."

"Quite the diet. Fresh vegetables and whole grain."

"I made up for it at the snack bar the next day. Ham and eggs, with butter on rye toast."

"Don't wannna let your cholesterol level drop too low."

"No."

We sat in the jeep, gazing at the busy restaurant. A row of glass windows was illuminated by bright interior bulbs but slathered with steam. Still, people could be made out walking back and forth and sitting at tables inside. "What makes you think she'll make contact with you here?"

"She told me she would." We waited. "She always said if we were ever separated and I wanted to reach her, I should come here and speak to the head chef. He's a cousin or something."

"Or *something*?" Ernie said.

"Not a lover," Strange said, "if that's what you're implying."

"Of course not," Ernie said sarcastically.

"She told me I should speak to him alone. So you guys are gonna have to sit here and wait."

"That's what we're good at," Ernie said.

I slid out of the passenger seat, tilted it forward, and Strange clambered out of the back seat. "Ten minutes," he said. "Might take a little longer if he's in the middle of a big order."

He waddled around the side of the restaurant, toward the back.

"Do you trust him?" Ernie asked.

"Not as far as I can throw him," I replied.

Ernie climbed out of the jeep, looped the security chain through the steering wheel tightly, and snapped shut the padlock. We followed the aroma of fish into darkness.

The stench was worse in the back; rotted fish flesh fermenting in brine. I stepped on something spongy. When I stopped and studied the sole of my shoe, a row of suction cups stared up at me. I brushed the tiny tentacle away. Ernie and I crouched behind a row of metal trash cans that seemed to contain every filthy corpuscle of rotting flesh from here to the Han River Estuary.

"I should've brought corks for my nostrils," Ernie said.

I waved my hand for him to be quiet.

Light and steam and the smell of burnt grease roiled out of the big double back doors of the restaurant. Overhead floodlights fought against thickening fog rolling in from the

Yellow Sea a few miles to the west. As we watched, two men hurried outside. Koreans, judging from their slim silhouettes. They trotted downhill to a short pier that extended into the gently lapping waters of the Han. One of them squatted by a stanchion while the other hopped into a small boat. As we watched, light flickered on in the boat and an internal combustion engine coughed to life.

"What the hell are they doing?" Ernie asked.

"Somebody's going somewhere."

"Not Strange."

"No," I agreed.

Suddenly, a half-dozen men, all wearing cook whites, emerged from the back of the restaurant. At their center, slightly taller than most of them, walked Sergeant First Class Cecil B. Harvey. He seemed reluctant to move forward but was being pushed by the weight of the crowd.

Ernie leapt to his feet, reaching inside his jacket for his shoulder holster as he marched toward the crowd. "Halt!" he shouted. And then "*Jeongji!*" which was Korean for the same thing. He pulled his .45 and started waving it, and I was about to join him as backup when footsteps pattered behind me. I turned in time to see the wicked blade of a chopping cleaver slash down toward me. I twisted to my left, and the sharp edge clanged uselessly onto the dented rim of an almost-full trash can. I fell backward, kicking to evade the figure in front of me and his glistening cleaver. He brandished it back and forth, taunting me, like a farmer preparing to harvest wheat. I slithered away from him, fumbling for the .45 tucked too snugly beneath my jacket.

The man raised the cleaver again.

A shot rang out.

The man with the meat cleaver grunted and stopped his advance. I took advantage of the delay to finally grab hold of the hilt of my pistol, freeing it from its leather holster. As I pulled back the slide, another shot fired, but this one went wide, and the man above me dropped his cleaver, turned, and staggered back toward the front of the restaurant. Suddenly, Ernie was crouching next to me.

"Don't you ever watch your *own* back?" he asked. "Why does it always have to be me?"

"Thanks," I said weakly.

The engine at the end of the pier growled. Ernie rose to his feet. "They're getting away."

I turned over on my hands and knees and looked. "Is Strange on the boat?"

"I think so."

Most of the men in cook's whites were sprinting back toward the restaurant. No overweight American with them. Ernie and I ran toward the pier, but it was too late to make a flying leap onto the fleeing boat. Maybe Errol Flynn could've managed it, but neither of us felt like taking a swim in the Han River.

In the darkness, staring at the receding craft, I could just make out a rotund figure standing next to the outboard motor. Strange. As we watched the boat speed away, Ernie said, "Crap!"

We hurried back toward the restaurant and barged into the kitchen. Keeping our hands on our firearms, we inspected everything as if we owned the place. The cooks were preoccupied with their work; chopping and sauteeing and steaming; paying no attention to the perspiring and, by now, rotten-fish-smelling Americans prowling amongst them. In Korean, I asked for a manager and everybody shrugged. We checked the front serving area and received the same cold shoulder. The man in cook whites who'd swung the cleaver at me seemed to have disappeared.

Just outside the front door, Ernie and I stopped to confer. "Strange is gone," I said, "that's clear. And nobody's talking."

"Mr. Kill could get 'em to talk," Ernie said.

"Yeah. I'll call him."

Ernie grabbed my elbow. "You sure you want to let him know what miserable failures we are?"

"I certainly don't. But what choice do we have?"

Ernie nodded, releasing my elbow.

Inside, at the reception counter, I found a phone resting on a knitted pad. I dialed Mr. Kill's number. Officer Oh answered. I told her, in English, where we were and that it appeared that Sergeant Harvey had been taken away by boat.

"Yes," she said.

I waited. When she added nothing, I said, "Well, aren't you going to do something about it?"

"Oh, yes."

"Well, what are you going to do?"

"Don't worry," she told me. "What's the term you Americans use? So clever." She paused. "Oh, yes, I remember. You say, 'We're already on it.'"

"On it? How?"

"The boat. The one Sergeant Harvey is traveling on. It is being monitored. Right now."

"Right now? As we speak?"

"Yes," she said. Paper rustled and I believe she was writing something down. "As we speak," she repeated, apparently quite proud of herself.

"Your English is getting better," I said.

"With your help," she replied.

"That's what I'm here for," I said.

I hung up. Helping people improve their English—and losing vital witnesses—seemed to be my two main claims to fame.

As it turned out, the traditional fishing boat we'd seen in the distance on the Han River behind the *nakji* restaurant was owned and manned by the Korean National Police. And it contained hidden but powerful state-of-the-art tracking equipment. So the little boat with the strong outboard motor that had left the pier with Strange aboard never actually had a chance of evading the KNPs. That didn't mean, however, that they'd intercept it. Rather, they would let it run where it was headed, hoping that it might lead them to the North Korean woman and her handlers. The vessel chugged steadily about three miles downriver, then pulled over just in front of the Haengju Bridge.

The KNPs alerted some patrol cars along the river, but unfortunately—and probably by design—the spot where the small boat had pulled over was difficult to access. No roads led to it, as it was wedged between facing cliffs and could normally only be reached on foot. By the time a couple of KNP patrol cars approached and the officers made their way to the landing spot, the boat was halfway back to its berth near Mapo. Whoever had been transported to Haengju had already departed the area.

Once again, Strange was in the wind, and where he had gone was a complete mystery to not only me and Ernie, but even to the Korean National Police.

-14-

The next morning, Ernie and I sat in the 8th Army Snack Bar staring at Strange's empty table. The entire Quonset hut was almost deserted, since 8th Army headquarters was being manned by only a handful of leftover GIs. The snack bar workers, including cooks, dishwashers, cashiers, and busboys, were off duty for the duration of Focus Lens. Until the five-thousand-some troops of the 8th Army headquarters returned from the field, all of Yongsan Compound was a ghost town.

Only one urn of coffee had been made, along with hot water for tea. A plastic fishbowl had been left beside the serving area with a sticker that read 25 CENTS. A handful of quarters and two loose dollar bills sat inside.

"So how do we find Strange?" Ernie asked.

I thought it over, and it came to me. "What would his North Korean handlers want most from him?"

"His charm and wit?"

I gave him a deadpan stare.

"Okay," Ernie said. "Not that. How about more information?"

"Right. And where is that classified information?"

Ernie sipped on his coffee. "In the classified documents cage."

"And since the MPs and every gate guard are watching for him, how would Strange ever be able to access that information?"

Ernie thought about it, then looked up at me. "Through Orting."

"Right. His man, Specialist Four Orting, is the only person besides you and me who's helped him during this entire caper."

"But Strange can't come on base."

"Right. So how would he contact Orting?"

"Telephone."

"Right again. So where's Orting now?"

"Probably over in the cage."

Even though 8th Army headquarters had ostensibly been transferred out into the field for the Focus Lens exercise, some functions were deemed too vital to move. These included communications with the Pentagon and the storage of top-secret documents. In a real war, of course, those functions would be moved, as would everything else but for just a practice exercise, it was deemed too risky to fiddle with them.

"Our man, Orting," Ernie said and started to stand.

"You wait here," I told him. "I'll go."

"But I'm better with GIs," he said.

"In some settings. Like the barracks."

"Or bars or poolrooms or nightclubs."

"Don't forget brothels," I said.

"Yeah, those too."

"But right now, Specialist Orting is operating in a formal military capacity."

"I can do that too," Ernie said, slightly offended.

I stared at him, waiting.

Nervously, he sipped his coffee. Finally he said, "Okay, Sergeant Smartypants. You go."

I finished my coffee, rose from the table, then walked outside of the quiet snack bar.

Orting stared at me from behind the barred window of the Classified Documents cage. He had a long face and intense eyes, and he appeared tired and worried.

"Running the whole show yourself?" I said.

"Yeah. What with Sergeant Harvey gone and Major Cranston out in the field, it's up to me to do everything. Log all the documents in and out, and worse, make decisions when these field-grade officers demand access to things when they're not listed on the need-to-know roster."

"Assholes, huh?"

"You said it. I'm the biggest idiot in the world, and they

always have a need that's greater than James Bond saving the world from nuclear holocaust."

I glanced up and down the carpeted hallway. The headquarters building was unusually silent. No one within earshot.

"When did he contact you?" I asked, leaning closer to the bars.

"What?"

"Sergeant Harvey. Did he call you this morning?" I knew Strange wouldn't worry about wiretaps since 8th Army didn't really have the technology to do it. As it was, they could barely keep the phones working.

"First thing. Before start of business. I wasn't even open yet."

"So you going to make the delivery yourself?"

His eyes widened. "How'd you know?"

"Strange and I work closely together."

"Who?"

"Sergeant Harvey. Strange is just a sort of codename we have for him." I gripped the cold iron bars. "He asked me to talk to you, make sure you're going to follow through."

Orting might be well-versed in classified paperwork, but he wasn't resistant to psychological manipulation.

"He wants me to." Orting ran long forefingers through straight brown hair. "Honestly, I don't know what to do."

"I can release you of the burden."

"I don't know," he said warily.

I pulled out my CID badge, flattened it, and slid it beneath the bars. "Law enforcement," I said. "Ongoing investigation. I'll even annotate that as the purpose on the checkout sheet. We'll list my name and badge number, and I'll sign and date. That lets you off the hook completely."

He thought about it, but I knew I had convinced him when he said, "What are you going to do with it?"

"That, you don't have a need to know. But suffice it to say that we're going to make sure that no more American units are attacked out at Focus Lens."

Orting grimaced. "God. Was that North Korean commandos?"

"That's what we believe."

"How could Sergeant Harvey have anything to do with that?"

"Believe it or not, we think he was trying to prevent it. In a misguided way."

Confused, Orting shook his head. "Above my paygrade." He turned, pulled out a ring of keys, and unlocked one of the cages behind him, then thumbed through a row of folders until he found the right one and slid it out. "Six pages," he said and read off the file number for me to write down on the checkout sheet. When we were done, I stuck the document beneath my shirt under my waistband, thanked him, and told him I would have it back as early as tomorrow. As I was walking away, I stopped and turned back to him.

"Oh, right. Where were you meeting him again?"

"Where else?" he said.

"Itaewon?"

He nodded. "The Hamilton Hotel Coffee Shop. Eight tonight."

I mimicked tipping my hat and turned and left.

In the glare of the lights in front of the Hamilton Hotel, a line of kimchi cabs waited for a fare, the drivers standing outside, smoking and gossiping and leaning against their cars. Inside, men in fancy jackets opened the front door for people entering; uniformed women behind the check-in counter bowed and greeted guests, and blue-smocked waitresses with white bandanas enveloping their straight black hair served hot drinks in the coffee shop.

Male and female customers, mostly Korean and mostly well-dressed, sat chatting and smoking and sipping on overpriced caffeine. Itaewon was a place of debauchery for American GIs, but the Hamilton Hotel right across the street was seen as an exciting and trendy place for the youthful elite of Seoul to congregate.

When Ernie and I entered with our blue jeans and sneakers and nylon jackets with dragons embroidered on the back, I leaned toward Ernie and said, "I feel as out of place as a tarantula on a wedding cake."

"Damn, that's good," he said, surprised. "You been taking clever pills?"

"No, it's a line from Raymond Chandler."

"Who?"

"Never mind."

The booths were made of varnished wood, low-backed so customers could have a private area but still be able to see and be seen. We found an open one and slid in.

The waitress approached and Ernie studied her. "Are you from North Korea?" he asked.

She didn't understand the English, so I translated. "No," she said, waving the flat of her palm to signal so.

"We're looking for someone from North Korea. A spy. Not you, right?"

I translated this too. Happily, since I'd just recently learned the Korean word for spy, which was *seupai*, direct from the English. Given their long, complicated, and somewhat Machiavellian history, Koreans would certainly have their own word for it, but if the derivative of the English word worked, that was good enough for me. My goal was to communicate, not impress some language professor.

The poor girl seemed totally confused now, so I gave her a break and asked her to bring two cups of coffee.

As she walked away, Ernie shouted after her. "And make sure it's overpriced!"

He didn't have to worry about that part. For a tiny cup of boiling water and a tablespoon of instant coffee, they charged 800 *won*. The equivalent of about $1.80, compared

WAR WOMEN ■ 199

to 25 cents on base. But Korea didn't grow coffee. Not even on their southernmost province of Cheju Island. So it all had to be imported. And since the Park Chung-hee regime considered coffee a luxury item, the customs tax was exorbitant. Which was why coffee in all forms, when purchased cheaply at the on-base commissary or PX, was such a hot item on the Korean black market.

The waitress brought two steaming cups on saucers, along with a small container of cream and a couple of packets of sugar. I sipped on mine and grimaced.

"Awful," I said.

"Just the way you like it," Ernie replied.

I set the cup down and studied the room once again. No one who looked like the North Korean woman I'd seen in the photograph in the hooch with that grandmother and her three grandchildren. I hoped they were still all right, but who knew?

And no Strange.

I resigned myself to wait and had just started back on my too-expensive cup of coffee when she walked in through the side door.

I wasn't the only person who turned to look. She was tall, with wavy black hair that curled where it reached her shoulders. Her lean body was draped in a knee-length overcoat and a flowered silk scarf was wrapped around her neck. Like a goddess from antiquity, she studied the people in the room.

I did my best to sit up straight and make myself presentable.

Then her eyes alighted on mine. No change of expression.

Ernie must've seen my mouth fall open.

"What?" he asked.

She walked toward us. I rose to my feet.

-15-

I gestured for the woman to join us. Without a word, she did, sliding into my side of the booth. I motioned for Ernie to scoot over so I could sit opposite her, mainly because I wanted to get a better view. For a second, it appeared as if she might smile at my discomfort, but being used to this reaction from men, the smile was stifled by boredom.

Ernie sipped on his coffee, confused by what he was witnessing. He was clearly thrown off-balance by my gawking.

I was unsure what to do next. No wonder fishermen had risked their lives to help her escape North Korea. No wonder Strange had risked his entire military career and even his freedom to get the information she wanted. And no wonder powerful men—likely North Korean agents—had seen her as useful in accomplishing their goals.

To test her English ability, I said, "Would you like some coffee?"

"Tea."

The waitress arrived, seeming somewhat surprised that a woman of apparent distinction had joined the table of two low-rent American GIs.

"*Ocha?*" the girl asked, using the honorific Japanese way of saying the word, which in Korean was merely *cha*. Was she hedging her bets, thinking her new customer might be Japanese? Whatever the reason, the woman once again nodded, and the waitress hurried away.

Ernie had been watching this show; a throwback, he must've thought, like a silent movie from the twenties, and he suddenly grew impatient.

"Who *are* you?" he asked. "Why did you come here?"

"Am I bothering you?" she asked in English.

Ernie jabbed his right thumb in my direction. "You're bothering *him*," he said. "Me, I'm okay. But we were expecting someone else. Someone who doesn't look anything like you."

"Sergeant Harvey," she said.

"Yeah. Him."

"He asked me to come."

"I'll bet."

Whether she understood the crude double entendre or not, she didn't show it.

The waitress brought the tea and set it in front of the woman. Steam rose from it, which partially blocked my view.

"Your name is Kim Yoon-jeong," I said.

She nodded, half smiling. "Your pronunciation is very good."

"Thank you."

Ernie glanced back and forth between us, incredulous at what kind of nut cases he was working with. "Can we knock off the mutual admiration and maybe get down to business sometime tonight?" he asked.

Using the fingertips of both hands, she lifted her handleless cup and sipped. Then she set it down and stared at Ernie expectantly. When he didn't say anything, she said, "Do you have a question?"

"Yes," Ernie replied. "Where is Sergeant Harvey?"

"He is safe."

"And why did you come here today instead of him?"

"To collect what he was promised."

"Which is?"

"A top-secret document."

She lifted her tea, amused, I thought, at our shocked reaction to her frankness.

"Do you have it?" she asked.

"Yes," I replied.

I'd read the document shortly after Specialist Orting had given it to me. It seemed innocuous at first, but the more I studied it, the more ominous it became. It was also about Focus Lens. But this time, instead of covering unit deployments in general, it covered only one specific type of deployment. Amphibious landings.

"You can't be serious?" Ernie said.

"What do you mean?" she asked.

"You don't expect us to just hand you a US Army classified document."

"Why not? Sergeant Harvey is indisposed."

"Indisposed how?"

She shrugged. It was an elegant movement. "Well," she said, setting her teacup down, "if you don't trust me, then I must be going."

"Strange," Ernie said. "We have to talk to him."

"Who?"

"Sergeant Harvey," I told her.

She stared at me curiously, giving me more attention than she'd given me since she walked through the door. "Is that what you call him? Strange?"

"Y-y-yeah," I stammered. "It's sort of a nickname."

She continued to study me, but in the end didn't ask anything more. Instead she said, "Without that document, your friend 'Strange' might become useless, even dangerous, to some very important people."

"Like who?"

She shrugged again. "People who are determined to disrupt, what is it called? Focus Lens."

"The North Koreans," Ernie said.

"Perhaps," she replied.

"What will they do to Strange?" I asked.

"Demand that he try again. To get the information he asked his subordinate to provide. Without it, having him around becomes a liability."

"They'll kill him?" Ernie said.

Through the steam rising from her teacup, she said, "What would you do?"

"Don't know. I can't think like a Commie."

The corners of her mouth upturned in the beginnings of a smile.

"Are you a Commie?" Ernie asked.

"Would I be here if I was? I risked everything to leave. But there's no escaping the Great Leader. His eyes and ears are everywhere. Now he has my mother and my children. I am only his servant." She leaned forward and stared into Ernie's eyes. "Doing what I'm ordered to do. Today, I've been told to get the document from you. If you don't give it to me, I won't pay the price but Sergeant Harvey will."

I reached beneath my shirt and touched the document. Ernie elbowed me in the ribs. No way was he going to participate in turning over a classified document to a North Korean go-between. Not in this lifetime. We were in deep enough as it was. Serving life in a federal penitentiary wouldn't do us or anyone else good.

I pulled my hand back. "Where's he being held?"

She coughed, looked back and forth between us, and took a long sip of her tea. When she saw that we weren't going to budge, she slid out of the booth, rose to her feet, and tightened the belt on her overcoat. After staring at us for a few seconds, giving us a last chance to recant, she turned and strode quickly toward the exit.

"Stop her," I told Ernie.

"Why? We're not giving her documents or anything else from Eighth Army."

"Then let's follow her," I said.

"Good idea."

We started to sidle out of the booth. Just then, a whistle shrilled.

The North Korean woman exited the door to the parking lot just as, on the opposite side of the room, a phalanx of blue-uniformed Korean National Policemen entered from the hotel lobby. They continued to sound their whistles, ordering everyone to stay in their seats. Within seconds, they reached our booth and surrounded us, four of them with hands on the hilts of their pistols. Behind them, someone approached. The uniformed officers made way as two Americans strode forward. We recognized them both.

Ernie groaned. "Not *you* two. What are you doing here?"

Our fellow 8th Army Criminal Investigation Agents, Jake Burrows and Felix Slabem, both pulled out their badges, let them fall open and held them in front of us. Burrows, the tall one, took the lead. "You're both under arrest."

"For *what*?" Ernie asked.

"For misappropriation of a classified document and attempted engagement in espionage with a foreign power."

"You must be out of your *freaking* mind."

When the shorter, more rotund Felix Slabem stepped toward me and started to pull out his handcuffs, I saw red. All I could think of was they were stopping me from both saving Strange and following Kim Yoon-jeong. All thanks to a couple of cretins who wouldn't know justice if it sneaked up and smacked them in their greasy chops.

I shoved Slabem backward. He rolled into the arms of the Korean cops behind him, and as they staggered under the jolt of his weight, I charged. Before I could make it to the door, they had caught up with me, and I was being wrestled by a half-dozen Korean cops, all of whom were smaller than me but determined. I swirled in a huge circle, tossing them around, struggling to get away. Ernie hopped up onto our table and then jumped to the next one. Women screamed, and with a leap that any swashbuckler would've been proud of, he landed in front of the door to the foyer, shoved through it, and sprinted. Jake Burrows and a few of the Korean cops followed, but given Ernie's fifteen-yard lead, my money was firmly on him.

I finally lost my balance and collapsed into a swarm of elbows and knees and cursing humanity. Despite my best efforts, I felt cold cuffs snap tightly around my twisted wrists.

■　■　■

The next morning, I sat forlornly in the locked interrogation room of the 8th Army Military Police station on Yongsan Compound. Last night, both Burrows and Slabem had crowed about their excellent police work. About how they'd pressured Specialist Orting into admitting that he'd allowed me to check out a classified document that I wasn't supposed to check out, and how he'd told me where and when to meet Sergeant Harvey.

"So we staked out the Hamilton Hotel," Slabem said. "Caught you totally flatfooted, and then we waited for Sergeant Harvey to show up. But instead, you guys had a conversation with some hooker. I guess she was too expensive for your blood, and when she left, you both got up to go. We weren't going to let you wander around Itaewon—"

"Because you never would've been able to keep up with us," I said.

He shrugged. "Whatever. So we decided to make the bust right there and then. It paid off."

He held up the classified folder Orting had given me. "Amphibious landings," he said. "What made you so interested in that all of a sudden?"

When I didn't answer, Slabem said, "Thinking of joining the marines?"

They found this so uproariously funny that they both guffawed for the better part of two minutes.

Of course, what the document was really about was the

landing of the US Marine Corps Expeditionary Force on the eastern shore of South Korea, just north of the city of Pohang. Part of the overall Focus Lens exercise. Whether or not Burrows and Slabem saw the import of this—that the North Koreans might want to know the where and when of the operation so they could disrupt this landing—I wasn't sure. But since I was locked up and facing court-martial, it was no longer my responsibility. It would be up to them and their superiors to decide what to do.

After gloating a little longer, but failing to get any real information out of me, they left.

I sat the rest of the night thinking about what I was facing, none of it good.

I'd misappropriated a classified document. I hadn't actually handed it to a North Korean agent, but a case could be made that I'd intended to pass it on to Strange who would, in turn, pass the information on to North Korean spies. Since a North Korean attack on the river-crossing unit had already occurred, they wouldn't go easy on me. Not in a military court-martial. Not with a jury composed of mostly high-ranking officers.

I started wondering which officer they would assign to defend me. According to military law, the defense counsel didn't have to be a lawyer. Any old commissioned officer would do. And usually they assigned an expendable second lieutenant—naïve, just out of training, and anxious to stay on the good side of his superiors. The smart move, when you were thrust into the maw of military jurisprudence, was to hire a civilian lawyer, one who'd actually fight for you.

Mentally, I went through my material assets. If I sold everything I owned and added that amount to my life's savings in the credit union on post, I'd be able to come up with maybe a little over three hundred dollars. Up that to five hundred after payday. Would that be enough to hire a stateside lawyer? Not even close. Maybe Katie Byrd Worthington knew an attorney who'd take my case on credit. Not that I had much. On my last stateside tour, I'd applied for a credit card and been turned down flat. No credit history, they told me, as if the fact that I'd never borrowed money made me somehow an undesirable.

Footsteps approached down the hallway. Somebody fumbled with keys, and then the door popped open. Grimes, an MP I'd worked with before. Rank of staff sergeant. A decent enough guy. He held a newspaper in his hand.

"Extra! Extra! Read all about it," he said. "Special edition of the *Oversexed Observer*." He tossed it to me. "Looks like you helped write it."

I caught it on the fly.

"Thanks," I said.

He nodded. "We'll bring you some chow in about a half hour."

"What about Burows and Slabem? Are they coming back?"

"Who knows?" Then he said, "Dorks," and shut the door.

Burrows and Slabem weren't popular amongst the military

police at 8th Army. Mainly because they conducted most of the internal investigations of our own law enforcement personnel and seemed to relish the duty.

The first page of the Flash edition of the *Overseas Observer* had a photograph of Corporal Hurley and the gals in her unit. Hurley held her .45 in the air, the other women pointed their M16 automatic rifles toward the sky. The headline said: WAR WOMEN BATTLE REDS. CASUALTIES COULD HAVE BEEN WORSE, CO SAYS.

I folded the paper. Great, now they were taking credit for chasing away North Korean commandos. I tried to calm down, and when I worked up my courage again, I opened the paper to page three. Another photo. This one of Staff Sergeant "Mule" Skinner hog-tied and hanging halfway out of the soju vendor's cart. The caption read: SEX FIEND CAPTURED BY WAR WOMEN.

Katie Byrd was laying it on thick. The 8th Army honchos would be livid. Especially when they received shocked inquiries from the brass at the Pentagon who'd want to know what the hell was going on over there in the ROK. The problem was that Katie Byrd was a civilian protected by the First Amendment. A bird in the bush. Nothing they could do about her. But me and Ernie had first been ordered to arrest her and then been ordered to facilitate her movements, and it didn't matter that we were just doing what we were told. Everything would be seen as our fault. And meanwhile, sitting here in the

MP station lockup, I was a bird in the proverbial hand. All the honchos had to do was tighten their grip, and my blood and guts would come seeping through their fingers. Ernie had done the smart thing because he wasn't a bird in the hand. Not at the moment, anyway. But eventually, he too would be caught in the army's vise-like squeeze.

Ernie had made good on his escape from the Hamilton Hotel Coffee Shop and was out there, free. What would he do? Get us both in deeper waste than we already were? Or maybe figure out a way to get us out of this mess? Could he find Strange before the North Koreans or whoever was holding him decided he was more of a liability than an asset?

I sat on the straight-backed chair in front of the scarred interrogation table, thinking. Finally becoming overwhelmed. I lay my head down, and for the first time in a long time, I prayed, clutching the *Overseas Observer* as if it were a rosary.

My breakfast was delivered, and although there's nothing quite as tasteless as cold scrambled eggs, I forced everything down: pulverized bacon, dry toast, even room-temperature coffee. When I was done, something scratched on my door like a wildcat trying to get in. When the scratching stopped, someone knocked, keys rattled, and it opened. Grimes again. He took my tray and whispered, "What you do is up to you. I scratched up the door lock to make it look like someone tampered with it. After that, I just say I don't know what happened."

He exited with the metal tray and utensils, but instead of closing and locking the door, he left it ajar. Was this a setup? I couldn't be sure, but I wasn't going to pass up the opportunity to escape. I had too much to do.

I stepped forward and peeked out into the hallway. Nobody. I tiptoed away from the MP Desk, where Grimes would be sitting, and walked as quietly as I was able through the winding passageways of the old ramshackle military police building. It was more than one building, really. A front Quonset hut, then some wooden additions, then another Quonset hut. All connected over the years with short walkways and tin roofs, everything coated over with inundation after inundation of olive-drab paint.

Footsteps pounded toward me and I ducked into the latrine. After the footsteps passed I peered out into the hallway and hurried toward a fire exit. I pushed through the door and emerged into sunlight. Quickly, I walked toward the Pedestrian Exit at Gate #5. Even though I didn't have my wallet or my military identification or my CID badge, or my .45, I knew the contract-hire Korean gate guard didn't check people exiting. Only entering.

I passed through the pedestrian gate a few yards away from the American MP, who was busy searching for contraband in the trunks of PX taxis.

Outside, I was free. Under KNP jurisdiction now, lost in the massive capital city of Seoul. The problem was that I had no money and, at the moment, nowhere to go. As I pondered this dilemma, a few yards behind me, a familiar voice spoke.

"'Bout time you got here."

Ernie.

I walked toward him. "Did you set that up?"

"Yeah. Grimes'll just claim that someone who's familiar with the MP station sneaked in through one of the unguarded entranceways and jimmied the door to the interrogation room. Easy when most everyone's out in the field. Besides, he has a grudge against Burrows and Slabem."

"A grudge for what?"

"Who knows? Those two guys would piss off the Pope. Come on, let's walk. Makes me nervous hanging around here."

We strolled toward the Samgakji Traffic Circle until we reached the shadows beneath the huge cement edifice. Cars and trucks roared above us. From there Ernie led me down a narrow side lane and finally to a tiny teahouse where the waitress bowed, seeming to know him.

"Cheap java," he said.

We sat at a rickety wooden table, and the waitress brought us two tiny cups of instant coffee.

"We have to find Strange," he said.

I nodded. "They could kill him at any time. However, for

the moment at least, they probably still see him as insurance. A human bargaining chip."

"Without that document, they don't know the precise landing positions," Ernie said. "Do you think they'll try striking anyway?"

"I believe they will. The US Marine Corps's landings on the east coast of Korea is just about the most spectacular operation of the entire Focus Lens exercise. More photogenic than the B52 overflights along the DMZ or the Seventh Fleet maneuvers off the coast of North Korea. This is what newspaper and TV guys love. Ships offshore, amphibious vehicles plowing through the waves, marines in full combat gear storming the beach. Great stuff."

"You've been hanging around Katie Byrd too long," he said.

"Don't I know it. But you've got to admit that international news coverage of Focus Lens must totally frost Kim Il-sung's balls."

"Yeah. So he'll want to throw a monkey wrench into the proceedings."

"Another one," I said. "He's already destroyed the pontoons at the Pyeongchang River."

"Okay. But without Strange's document, how will the North Koreans figure out where the landing is going to be, much less set up a plan to disrupt it? There's a lot of beachfront property on the east coast. Plenty of prime landing spots."

"There are other ways. First of all, the Public Affairs Office will have to know where to direct the TV cameras and reporters. They'll probably have transportation lined up for them."

"Primo publicity for the Department of Defense. So they'll drive the reporters there in army buses on the day of the landing."

"Right. And the medical people. They'll have to know where to bring their ambulances and other rescue equipment. Somebody always gets hurt in a big operation like this. They'll have to be ready. If there's a serious accident, like one of the landing craft turns over in rough seas, they'll need plenty of help standing by."

"And overhead choppers," Ernie added.

"And logistics support we haven't even thought of. So if the North Koreans can't get the document, the Commies will just ferret out the information the old-fashioned way: person to person. You saw her. Do you think that North Korean woman could get information out of an American GI?"

"She could suck him dry of every fact he ever knew," Ernie replied.

"And facts he doesn't even *know* he knows. Whether he's a private or a general."

"Especially if he's a general," Ernie said. "Ego stroking. Makes him an easy target."

I sipped on my coffee. The instant they used must've been purchased some time during the Stone Age. I could run my tongue around each individual "soluble crystal," as Madison

Avenue liked to call them. These must've already fossilized. I set my cup down.

"So the North Koreans will get the information somehow and use it to set up some sort of sabotage operation like they did with the pontoon barges."

"Right."

"But what good does this do us? We have no idea where Strange is being held. Nor do we know the location of this North Korean woman or her family."

"Did you believe her when she said she was being extorted?"

"Yes."

"Why?"

"Like she said, the Great Leader has long tentacles."

"And suction cups that drink blood."

We sat in silence for a while, both of us trying to think of a way to find Strange. I gazed out the dirty front window. Across the narrow pathway, another faded sign advertised another rundown shop. I could barely make out the *hangul* lettering: *haemul*. Seafood. Next to the lettering was a splotchy blue drawing of a flapping fish.

Then I realized where we should search. I pointed toward the sign. Ernie studied it. "Yeah, so what? There must be a million seafood eateries in Seoul."

"Right. But only one place the vendors themselves can buy fresh fish."

He gazed at me. "Only one?"

"Mandated by the government," I told him. "So they can regulate the sale and tax it and make sure the local population isn't poisoned."

"You mean all the chefs and people who sell seafood have to go to a single market to buy their product?"

"Every morning. Early. Their customers are very particular."

Koreans were a seafaring people. Their mountainous country not only featured many freshwater rivers, but over 3,000 offshore islands. They'd been harvesting the bounty of the sea since before the beginning of recorded history.

Ernie didn't like the idea of us staking out the fish market because he was revolted by even the thought of acres of smelly, slimy things all in one location. But he was unable to come up with a better place to start our search, even after thinking on it for a while. So my plan won out.

It was still pitch-black in the fog-shrouded predawn morning. Ernie'd groaned when I rose from my cotton-filled mat in the little *yoin-suk*, where we'd rented space in the community sleeping room. I used the bathroom first and then he took his turn. Within ten minutes, our faces were washed, though not shaven since we didn't have razors—and we were outside in the cold damp air, traipsing toward the main road. Eventually, an early bird taxi flashed his lights and we waved him down.

"*Odi?*" the driver asked.

"Noryangjin Shijang," I told him. The Noryangjin Market.

His eyes widened. "You like fish?" he asked in English.

"Yeah," Ernie growled. "We freaking love fish. The slimier the better. Crazy about them."

The cabbie shut up and drove.

-16-

It was a huge place, covered by thick wooden stanchions holding up a massive tin roof. The flooring was cement with regularly spaced metal-grate drains, and most of the vendors wore knee-high rubber boots and spent plenty of time hosing down their area to make it look presentable. Seafood of all types was piled atop mounds of blue ice. Glossy eyeballs and sparkling fins created an atmosphere of sea-salted life, almost caught in mid-swim as it swirled madly through teeming oceans.

Salesmen shouted, some of them using bullhorns, waving in customers. Easels held blackboards, which were marked with almost indecipherable multihued lettering advertising prices per kilo that had periodically been erased with woolen sleeves and chalked over again with the latest quote.

When we reached the *nakji* section, Ernie balked. "I'm not going in there," he said, pointing to a translucent plastic screen that divided the octopus sales area from the scaled fish area.

"You don't have to," I told him. "Let's just find someplace we can watch from. See but not be seen."

We found it, between two trucks on the edge of the loading ramp. Fluorescent lights hung low over the wooden platforms that held the octopus and next to that the squid. Shoppers, mostly men, wandered through the stands, occasionally stopping to squabble with a vendor over the price per kilo, but deals were struck quickly. These people were bulk buyers. They not only knew a fair price when they saw it, but normally had a number of products to buy and little time to get back to their restaurant or their retail outlet. The day's preparation had to be started.

We stood for over a half hour, quickly growing tired of the cold and damp and invasive penetration of the enveloping aroma of fish. That's when I heard it. Something being chopped on wood.

I stared, hardly trusting my eyesight. A man who had been examining an octopus grabbed one and lay it flat on a chopping block, then pulled out his own meat cleaver and chopped down and sliced it clean in two. He leaned forward, examined the innards and, seemingly satisfied, started haggling with the *nakji* vendor.

I nudged Ernie. "You recognize that guy?"

"Which guy?"

"The guy in the middle of those octopus tables. The one in the white cap."

Ernie squinted. "Never seen him before in my life."

"Yes, you have," I said. "In fact, you tried to kill him."

Ernie's mouth fell slightly open. "I did?" And then he remembered. "Oh, *that* guy. The one with the cleaver, trying to slice your head open."

"Yeah, him. You missed with that shot, but it was enough to convince him to run away."

Ernie grinned broadly. "Saved your life."

"You almost lost it by missing. If that guy had been a little more bold, he might've taken another whack at me."

"No way. He knew old Dead-Eye Bascom had drawn a bead on him."

Money exchanged hands, and the vendor wrapped a football-sized mound of *nakji* in newspaper and then knotted it securely with string. Afterward, he stuffed it in a plastic bag.

The man in the white cap accepted his purchase, turned, and started walking toward the front of the fish market. We followed, and he eventually jumped into the passenger seat of a three-wheeled truck with the logo of the Hamhung Seafood Emporium printed on the side.

Ernie sprinted for a cab, and even though we'd already lost sight of the truck, the driver was able to find them again at the onramp to the main road headed toward the center of the city.

Once we were following comfortably, Ernie said, "This ought to be interesting."

"Yeah. Even more interesting if I still had my weapon."

"I've still got mine," Ernie replied, patting the left front of his nylon jacket.

And he still had his military ID, his CID badge, and a few dollars in his pocket. How I envied him. I tugged on my loose waistband. They'd even taken away my belt.

The truck parked in back of a large eatery featuring noodles and seafood. It was in Pongnae-dong, a working-class area of Seoul, only walking distance from Seoul-*yok*, the main train station. It made sense that they'd choose to locate here, since commuters could stop on their way to or from work for a cheap but nutritious hot meal.

I found a pay phone, dropped in one of Ernie's hundred-*won* coins, and dialed the KNP headquarters. Officer Oh answered. I identified myself and told her where I was and explained that we'd located one of the men who'd attacked us on the banks of the Han River and thereby helped with the abduction of Sergeant First Class Harvey. She understood the import right away. If we could arrest this man and his associates, they might very well be able to lead us to not only the whereabouts of Strange, but the suspected North Korean agents who were holding him.

"How many men do you need?" she asked.

"Ten or more," I told her. "It's a large restaurant. Best if we surround it first and then enter in force and take everyone down at once."

"Yes, yes. I will speak to Inspector Gil immediately. It could take us twenty minutes, maybe more. We'll be there as soon as we can."

She hung up.

I returned to Ernie's hiding place in an alley nearby.

"Something's up," he said.

"What?"

"I think they spotted me. Or spotted us when we were tailing them. That cabbie wasn't too careful."

"He's not a professional," I said.

"A few people have been looking out that side window there." He pointed. "I don't think they've seen us here yet, but the point is, they're looking."

"Officer Oh's putting together a response team right now, but it could take twenty minutes."

"With that much time, they could sneak out the back," Ernie said.

A group of school children appeared at the intersection at the far end of the building. The boys wore brightly colored orange caps with short brims, and the girls, pin-on hats of the same color. The uniform was white shirts or blouses and beige pants or skirts. As they marched, they strode forward happily until they came to the stop at the intersection where, one by one, each child bumped into the child in front of them. They must've been six or seven years old. In front, a tall boy and a tall girl each waved a matching orange pennant with lettering I couldn't make out. Two female teachers hovered about, waving their hands and cooing instructions, coaxing the rambunctious children back into line.

"Field trip," Ernie said. "On their way to the train station."

Just then, three men emerged from the front of the noodle shop. One of them was the man with the meat cleaver, but he was wearing a warm overcoat now and had gotten rid of his white cap. Another tall Korean man had a firm grip on the man wedged between them. That man, looking like he was about to hurl, was our quarry, Sergeant First Class Cecil B. Harvey.

"Got him," Ernie said. He reached for his .45.

"Hold it," I said, grabbing his fist. "You can't use that. There are children here."

The pedestrian light changed, and the parade of students started across the intersection. Strange and his captors rushed forward, quickly catching up with the kids and staying abreast of them. Once they reached the far side of the intersection, there was a taxi stand with a queue of about a half-dozen commuters. The men seemed to be almost dragging Strange along, but they managed to pass the line of children and shoved their way to the front of the taxi line. Despite protests, they ushered Strange into the back seat of the first taxi.

"Oh no, they don't!" Ernie shouted and took off running.

He was gone before I was able to react, so all I could do was follow.

When Ernie hit the line of kids, he gently pushed past them, trying not to run anyone over. When he reached the cab, Strange and one of his captors were in the back seat, but the man with the overcoat was still standing guard outside. He reached in one of the pockets and pulled out his meat cleaver. Ernie's momentum kept him moving forward, and when the man swung the thick blade, I thought for sure he was going to hack off at least an arm if not slash Ernie's fool neck, but Ernie surprised me and twisted at the last moment. The wicked blade flashed in the morning sunlight and slammed into the hood of the taxicab. Slowly, the raised radio antenna tilted over and fell off.

Children screamed. The teachers rushed forward, trying to shoo the kids away from danger, but once panicked, they were either standing frozen, staring at Ernie and the man with the meat cleaver, or running off in all directions, heedless of the vehicular traffic that was still streaming by. I hopped my way through the churning crowd and ran directly at the man with the cleaver. By now Ernie had pulled his .45 and aimed it at the man's face. The cleaver guy was so focused on the business end of Ernie's pistol that he never saw me coming. I tackled him, head down, shoulders plowing into his side. He crumpled against the side of the taxi, and then I pulled him almost upright, twisted him, and slammed him onto the muddy cement. His head cracked on blacktop, and the meat cleaver dropped from his hand. I kicked it into a storm drain, and by now Ernie had opened the front seat of the cab and was pointing his .45 at the tall Korean man in the back, who climbed out of the far door and took off running.

Given the liberal rules of engagement observed by both the Korean government and the 8th United States Army, Ernie could've popped a cap at the fleeing man. But there were too many children behind us and too many civilians in front of us, so he didn't take the chance. He held his fire.

Sirens sounded in the distance, growing louder.

In seconds, we were surrounded by Korean National Police. Officer Oh approached and asked us if anyone was hurt. I pointed at the meat cleaver man lying in the gutter. She barked an order, and two officers lifted him and took him away.

She studied the children cowering against the wall of the brick building opposite us. The teachers were trying to get them back in line while at the same time comforting the ones who were crying, which was most of them. The ones who weren't, appeared to be in shock.

She looked up at me, waiting for an explanation.

"Sorry," I said. "No choice."

She nodded and looked back at the children, placing her hands on her hips and sighing.

After the meat cleaver guy had been taken into custody, Officer Oh ordered the noodle shop to be thoroughly searched. In the basement, they found evidence that it had been occupied: sleeping mats and leftover ramen wrappers, even a plastic giraffe apparently abandoned by a toddler. But Kim Yoon-jeong's family, her mother and her three children, were nowhere to be found.

"This group might still strike at the Focus Lens exercise," Officer Oh said.

Back at KNP headquarters, the first couple of hours of Meat Cleaver Man's interrogation elicited nothing. He was a particularly tough nut to crack, and it was thought that he'd undergone special training in North Korea.

"Plus," Officer Oh told us, "he has the added incentive of knowing that three generations of his family back home will be given a life sentence in one of the Great Leader's prison camps if he cooperates with us." She walked out of the room at the sound of a phone ringing.

So Mr. Shin and Kim Yoon-jeong were still at large. Strange didn't know where they were, but he confirmed what they planned to do.

"Disrupt an amphibious landing," he said.

"How do you know?"

"They kept asking me about Katie Byrd and the other reporters and when they would be going to the east coast."

"They want international media coverage."

"Yes."

"What'd you tell them?"

"I only told them what I knew from one of the first classified documents."

"A document Mr. Shin must've read too," I said.

"Of course he did. It gives the time and place of the Marine Corps landing."

"Which is?"

Strange tilted his head and looked at me. "Didn't you read it?"

"At the time," I told him, "I didn't have a need to know."

He shrugged and gave me the information about a beach north of Pohang on the east coast. From the more updated document that I'd received from Orting, the originally planned time and place hadn't been changed.

"Miss Kim is terrified of Mr. Shin," Strange said. "Always has been. Long before I figured out what was going on."

"And what *is* going on?" I asked.

"These people are fanatical followers of the Great Leader. They're willing to sacrifice themselves, her, and her mother and children, all for the cause."

"Not to mention you."

"In their minds, I don't even count as a sacrifice." A slight smile twisted his thin lips. "Neither do you two," he added. "Nor Katie Byrd Worthington. Nor any long-nosed *miguk-nom*."

American lout.

"What do we count as?" Ernie asked.

"Enemies," Strange replied.

Just then, Officer Oh returned to the interrogation room and told me I had a phone call. I followed her down the hallway to another office and picked up the receiver.

"Where the hell are you?" a voice shrilled. It was Katie Byrd.

"Doing my job," I replied.

"The *hell* you are. Your job is to be escorting me concerning this war women story, à la orders from General Frankenton, in case you forgot."

"I didn't forget. When we let you off at the Bando, you took off without a word."

"I want you both back here now. With your jeep and a full tank of gas."

"Why?"

"Because I *say* so, that's why. And because some cretin battalion commander at Camp Long has gone back on his word, and he's trying to treat my girls as common *criminals!*"

I held the receiver away from my ear. Officer Oh had taken a seat behind her desk, looking worried.

"It'll take us a while," I said.

"*Why?*"

"In case you haven't heard, Ernie and I are fugitives now."

"About time. Do you still have access to your jeep?"

"I believe so."

"Then get your butts over here in an hour. I'll be waiting out front."

With that she slammed down the phone.

I set the receiver in the cradle and gazed sheepishly at Officer Oh.

"She's a little excitable."

"'Excitable,'" Officer Oh repeated, grabbing her English-Korean dictionary and thumbing through it quickly. She ran her forefinger down the page, stopped, and a few seconds later looked up at me.

"Yes, 'excitable.'" Then she smiled. "Miss Katie Byrd very *excitable.*"

-17-

On the night we met Kim Yoon-jeong at the Hamilton Hotel, Ernie had hidden his jeep in what he hoped was a secure area near the open-air Itaewon Market. He'd paid one of the produce vendors to keep it under wraps beneath a huge tarp. When we pulled the canvas back, Ernie inspected the jeep and found everything in order.

The amphibious landing of the United States Marine Corps Expeditionary Force was scheduled for 0700 hours the following morning at a place about thirty klicks north of the east coast city of Pohang at a beach called Namho. We felt it was unlikely that the place and time would be changed at this point, despite the marauding band of North Korean commandos who'd blown up the bridge-crossing pontoons. Too much time and money would be at risk now. Besides, an entire brigade of ROK Army infantry had been deployed to protect the perimeter surrounding the landing zone. Nothing and nobody could penetrate that barrier, highly trained commandos or not.

At least, that was the working assumption.

Given the massiveness of the defensive preparations, it seemed likely that even if 8th Army made some last-minute changes, Mr. Shin and his minions would be able to gather enough intelligence to pinpoint the location of the amphibious landing. And who knew what they'd be able to pull off? Probably nothing. Still, we had to prepare for the worst.

After Ernie started the engine, I climbed into the passenger seat, Strange in back.

Ernie checked his wristwatch. "It is currently eleven hundred hours. We have about a hundred and fifty kilometers to travel and twenty hours to get there."

"Plenty of time," Strange said.

"Yeah. Normally. But you forget that we're still considered fugitives. All three of us."

"Even *me*?" Strange whined.

"Especially you, butthead. You're the guy who started all this."

"I didn't have any *choice*."

"Tell it to the judge. And to make matters worse, during Focus Lens, security is always high. And with a North Korean attack on the pontoon unit making everybody nervous, you can figure that every guard and sentry and military policeman from here to Pohang will have their weapon loaded and their finger on the trigger, and they'll be ready to blast anyone who looks at them cross-eyed."

"I'll keep my shades on," Strange said.

"I think you're missing the point," I replied.

"No, I'm not. I get it. But what choice do we have? We have to get there and stop these guys."

Ernie turned in his seat and looked at him. "You've suddenly developed a soft spot for the Marine Corps?"

"No. I mean, yes. But only as far as it concerns Miss Kim."

"You call her 'Miss,' even though she's a widow?"

"She's a miss to me."

"A hit and a miss," Ernie said, turning back around. He shoved the jeep in gear.

We rolled forward, only one pistol between the three of us. Me with no identification, no badge, no weapon, not even a belt. Strange, however, through all the mayhem, had somehow held on to his dark glasses and his cigarette holder. Maybe he kept spares jammed up his rectum.

Ernie turned left on the MSR and a half mile later hung a right heading toward Namsan Tunnel Number Three.

"Hey," Strange protested. "To cross the Han River you should've turned left."

"Don't you think I know that?" Ernie growled.

"Then why are we going downtown?"

"To pick up a friend of ours," I told him, "at the world-famous Bando Hotel."

Strange groaned. "Not Katie Byrd," he whined.

"Her exactly."

"She'll get us all killed," he said.

I shrugged. "At least we'll die in the cause of truth, justice, and the American way."

Strange leaned forward in his seat. "It's the *Oversexed Observer* we're talking about here."

"Sort of like the Bill of Rights," Ernie said. "A founding document."

Katie was waiting for us in front of the Bando, decked out in her jungle khakis with her canvas camera bag strapped over her shoulder. She hopped in the back seat next to Strange and shouted, "Camp Long, Wonju. *Balli balli!*" As if she were shouting orders at a cab driver.

Ernie ignored her and shoved the jeep in gear, rolling out into the midmorning Seoul traffic.

"No hello or anything," I said, turning around to look at her.

"Hello," she barked.

I motioned toward Strange. "You've met Sergeant First Class Harvey?"

"Only by reputation," she said, turning away from him.

"So what's going on at Camp Long?" I asked.

She slid the strap of her camera bag off her narrow shoulder and clunked it down on the metal floor between her feet.

"Ansel P. Lancorn. That's his name. Lieutenant colonel and commander of the combat engineer battalion at Camp Long. And a complete asshole."

"You have to be an asshole," Ernie said, "to command a battalion. Prerequisite."

"He promised Corporal Hurley and all the women who'd taken matters in their own hands out in the field that all their statements would be taken by a JAG officer who was flying in from the Nineteenth Support Group at Camp Henry. He even had somebody chopper in, carrying a briefcase. Turned out it wasn't a JAG officer at all but a medical officer from the 121st Evac who was going to be checking all the women for sexually transmitted disease. 'To protect his men,' Landcorny said."

"'Landcorny?'" I asked.

"That's what Hurley and the girls call him. And while they were still thinking the newly arrived officer was from JAG, they turned their weapons in to the arms room, and about five minutes later, Landcorny had them marched over to the dispensary, and now they're locked up and jammed together in the waiting room with armed MPs making sure they don't go anywhere."

"How'd they get in touch with you?" Ernie asked.

"Hurley slipped my phone number to one of the Korean waitresses who works at the Camp Long Officers Club. Apparently, they're friends."

"They must be good friends," Strange added, "for her to be risking her job like this."

I glared at him, warning him to keep his trap shut. He sunk back against Ernie's tuck-and-roll.

By now we'd reached the Seoul to Pusan Highway and Ernie merged into traffic that was moving at a much faster clip. This road would take us south and before we reached the Osan Air Force Base turnoff, we'd hang a left at the big intersection that headed east toward Wonju.

"So they're temporarily detained," I told Katie Byrd. "Any idea what moves he plans to take next?"

"None."

"And what are we going to do about it?"

"I've already done it."

Uh-oh, I thought. Even Ernie's shoulders tensed.

In a hoarse whisper, I asked, "What did you do?"

Katie sat up straighter. "I called Frankie Baby, of course. He was mad as hell. I told him you two are driving me out there, and he estimated we should arrive about thirteen hundred hours. He says he'll fly to Camp Long and meet us there."

"Deus ex machina," I said.

"What?"

"Never mind. Sounds like you've solved the problem."

"I hope so," Katie Byrd said, determination quivering in her voice.

I turned around and seated myself properly, settling in for the long drive. Ernie glanced over at me, a pained expression on his face. I could guess what he was feeling. When generals and colonels are being moved around like chess pieces, even by a civilian, enlisted men tend to get nervous. For us, it is like mortals attempting to manipulate gods. The ancient Greeks would've known we were heading for trouble.

When we arrived at the front gate of Camp Long, General Frankenton's 8th Army Command helicopter was already sitting on the helipad. The MPs raised the barrier for us and at the same time called ahead. General Frankenton's female adjutant, the one we'd seen out at the field headquarters, was standing outside the Camp Long operations building. She escorted Katie Byrd inside. Since she didn't tell us to wait outside, Ernie and I followed. Instead of being ushered into a conference room or somebody's office, she led us to the employees' break room. Colonel Lancorn and General Frankenton were sitting at a small round table across from each other, laughing and drinking coffee like two old friends.

General Frankenton seemed delighted when he saw Katie Byrd. "Come on in. Come on in. Have a seat. Coffee?"

"No, thank you," Katie said primly, lowering herself into one of the folding chairs. "How about the women of the transportation unit?" she asked without preamble. "Have they been released from confinement?"

She pulled out her notebook while at the same time glaring at Colonel Lancorn. He grinned more broadly as if privy to some tremendous joke.

"I wouldn't call it confinement," General Frankenton said.

"Just a checkup is all. I was telling the colonel here that you can't keep a good woman locked up for long. Isn't that true, Lancorn?"

"Yes, sir."

"Where are the women now?" Katie asked.

"In the dispensary," Lancorn interjected. "Waiting for their lab results."

"To see whether or not they have VD?"

"Got to keep the troops healthy," Lancorn replied.

"What troops? Keep the male troops healthy by cleansing the women? What about Skinner? What about the other lowlifes who assaulted women out there during your precious field exercise? An exercise that ended in miserable failure, I might add."

Ernie and I glanced at each other. Katie sure knew how to ruin a jocular reunion.

"Their problem isn't physical," Katie went on. "Their problem is that they were victims of a series of brutal assaults."

General Frankenton frowned. "'Brutal' is a harsh word, isn't it, Katie Byrd? Some boys got carried away because of these ladies' charms, isn't that what it is?"

Katie'd had enough. She stood up. "I'm not playing this old-boy routine with you, Frankie Baby. You either start taking these allegations seriously or your dancing skills or lack thereof will be plastered all over the front page of next week's *Overseas Observer*. Or maybe we won't even wait until Sunday.

The film has already been processed in the lab. Maybe we'll move up the pub date."

"Film?" General Frankenton said. "You mean *this*?"

From the front pocket of his fatigue shirt, he pulled out a gray plastic cylinder, popped the cap, and then began to unroll a long strand of cellulose until it fell to the floor.

Katie's mouth fell open.

"A secret military conference between allied nations," Frankenton said. "Me and the South Koreans, discussing defense research and development. Vital to our national interests. Exposing such classified proceedings could be a violation of the espionage act. Even for an illustrious reporter like yourself, Katie Byrd. The Hong Kong authorities agreed. In fact, they accompanied our embassy personnel during the raid on your offices in that rundown six-story building on a back street near the Wan Chai district. They were very thorough, Katie. All prints and copies were scooped up. They sent me this," he said, holding up the now-empty film container, "as a souvenir."

Katie took the hit without flinching. She adjusted the strap on her camera bag. "Okay, Frankie. You've got the film. I'm sure those two *kisaeng* you were tormenting with those chopsticks will be happy it won't be published. Grateful that their mothers won't see what depravity they were forced into."

Colonel Lancorn turned toward the general as if to say, "Do you want me to slap her?"

Frankenton ignored him.

Katie continued. "None of this means that the women of the 877th shouldn't be treated fairly. They were attacked by Staff Sergeant Skinner and at least a half dozen of the other creeps in that unit. Their company commander ignored the problem, looked the other way, called the whole thing nothing more than a he-said-she-said situation. Someday the army's going to have to face the fact that without a draft you're not going to be able to fill the ranks with men only. Women are required and needed to bolster our national defense. And as long as they're courageous enough to take the oath of enlistment, they deserve fair treatment once they're in."

This seemed to enrage General Frankenton. His brow furrowed and he leaned forward as if trying to force Katie Byrd to take a step backward. She didn't move.

"They'll be treated fairly," he said. "Once finished with the checkup, they'll be moved out to the Nineteenth Support Command headquarters where they will be deposed, one-by-one, in a formal hearing. When all the evidence is gathered, a judgment as to how, or if, to go forward with sexual assault prosecutions will be made. But not until then."

"You better treat them right, Frankie Baby," she told him, "or you'll never be rid of me."

Like an Old West gunslinger, Katie pulled her camera out of her bag, aimed it, twisted the focus, and flashed a photo of the two surprised men. Colonel Lancorn said, "Hey!" but

Katie was out the door, Ernie and me following close on her heels.

Outside, Katie stood on the broad wooden porch in front of the headquarters, as if catching her breath. "Where's the dispensary?" she asked.

About fifty yards across the parade field, the roof of a single-story building was marked with a red cross on a white background. "There," I said, pointing.

At that moment, out of the side door of the dispensary, soldiers started to file out. As they formed up as a group I realized that they were all women.

"Hurley," Katie said. "All of them."

"They're sticking together," I said.

"Smart," Ernie added.

As they executed a right face and started to march across the parade ground, more soldiers appeared in doorways and in windows. Men. All of them. When the women had just about reached the flagpole in front of the command building, the men started hooting. "I got something for ya', baby," one of them shouted, grabbing his crotch. And then more were shouting obscenities and laughing, the cackling and brazenness gradually increasing as the women made their way toward Katie. Hurley stopped in front of us and ordered the formation to halt.

"Katie," she said, "you kept your word."

Katie Byrd tried to say something but her voice just

croaked. Fiercely, she wiped moisture from her eyes. I helped her down the steps and Hurley enveloped her in a hug, then the women broke ranks and were all walking away, arms around one another. The men kept yapping and barking and howling.

"Baboons," Ernie said.

Occasionally, one of the war women raised her hand and flipped the bird toward the chorus of chattering apes. That's when I realized that Hurley was leading Katie Byrd and all of the war women toward a sign marked: BATTALION ARMS ROOM.

"Holy shit," Ernie said.

By the time Ernie and I made our way inside the thick cement-walled building, the armorer was holding up his hands defensively and shaking his head from side to side.

"Not authorized," he said.

He spoke in a thick Bostonian accent so the "h" in "authorized" was barely pronounced.

Ernie turned to me and said, "Not auto-rized."

Most civilians don't realize that the military has almost total gun control. When you enter basic training the officers in charge are not about to hand a bunch of knuckleheaded teenagers assault rifles and magazines loaded with lethal ammunition. Any eighteen-year-old civilian might be able to purchase those things at his local hardware store and walk out without a care in the world. But not in the army. First, you will be trained. Only then, once the drill sergeants have taught you the difference between your butthole and the business end of an M16 rifle, will you be allowed to lock and load live ammunition and point your weapon downrange. A process that usually takes at least four weeks. And even then, you can only check out your weapon from the vault-like arms room when authorized by your unit commander.

The armorer was a little guy with a big metal ring of keys clipped to his hip. The girls surrounded him, some of them cooing and stroking his hair to calm him down; others kneeling and trying to figure out how the metal clip worked. The armorer kept backing up until he was pressed against the metal mesh of the arms room cage, and then somebody snatched his keys. He protested, but the crowd flowed away from him and the door below the sign that said ISSUE was unlocked. Hurley hopped inside and started grabbing each woman's individually issued weapons card, exchanging them for the rifle that corresponded to their rack number.

Then she started passing out ammo and magazines.

I sidled as close as I could through the crowd, and during a slight delay in the action, I shouted at Hurley, "What are you going to do?"

She turned, wiping a strand of hair from her face. "The main thing is that we're not going to allow these jerks to take us into custody ever again. Even for a physical. We'll be armed and in our own barracks. We'll mount our own perimeter guard at night, and *Landcorny* can negotiate with us the next time he decides to have us checked for VD, treating us as if we're a herd of livestock."

"You're not allowed to check out weapons and ammo unless your unit commander authorizes it," I said.

She stopped and glared at me. "Don't you think I *know* that? I also know that we're sick and tired of being pushed around and treated as if there's something wrong with us when there's actually something wrong with *them*. All those stinking men who think that we're their personal property."

She let someone else take over the issuing of the M16 rifles and stepped closer to me and Ernie. "Back at the dispensary," she said, "we voted on it. We're all going to stick together. And either we win together or we lose together. Either way, we fight."

Katie Byrd was busy taking notes and snapping photos. Some of the shots were posed, most of them of the women grabbing their weapons, breaking them into component parts to make sure they were clean and serviceable, and running rods through the barrels to wipe out dirt and oil that might've been picked up while they were out in the field.

Someone had found a clipboard and attached a clean pad of writing paper to it. The women were writing down their names and ranks and the names of their next-of-kin back in the United States, including phone numbers and addresses. At the top, someone had written: *For Katie Byrd and the Overseas Observer.*

When she had a free moment, I pulled Katie aside. She told me that she was staying here with the war women and we were free to move on to the amphibious landing site if we wished.

"Don't you want to report on it?"

She shrugged. "There'll be plenty of press there. *This*," she said, pointing to the floor, "is my exclusive."

"Maybe the story of your career," I said.

"Or of my life."

-18-

Ernie, Strange, and I slipped away from Camp Long.

I felt bad about leaving Katie and Corporal Hurley and all the women to the whims of Colonel Lancorn, and the abuse of the simian horde, but I felt a little less bad when the general's command chopper lifted into the air just as we exited the front gate of Camp Long.

We used side roads, little dirt lanes that didn't have American MP checkpoints. Unfortunately, they did have ROK Army checkpoints. But Ernie's CID badge and emergency dispatch, which was printed in both English and Korean, bluffed us through each of those. However, a farmer in one village where we stopped to buy a couple of liters of gasoline told us that there was a major roadblock up ahead, strategically placed at a bend in the road so you'd be on top of it before you had a chance to turn around. It was just past the top of a mountainous ridge that led down toward the Namho Beach. And he said there were at least a couple of American MPs.

"It figures they'd put one there," Ernie said. "On the final ridge, as a last line of defense before the amphibious landing area."

"It's not gonna fly, me being without identification," I said. "We can bluff the Koreans but not the American MPs."

"Shin let me keep mine," Strange said, almost as if he were proud of that accomplishment.

"Why?" I asked.

"He likes me."

"*Likes* you?"

"Yeah. That's what he said. Before, when I kept saying that Koreans would never get anywhere because they were always fighting each other, he was pissed at me. But now, after all he's been through trying to stop the 'invasion,' as he calls Focus Lens, he realized finally that I might be right."

"You guys had a long heart-to-heart, huh?" Ernie asked.

"Plenty of time. Nothing to do but eat fish."

"How many fighters is he planning on bringing with him?"

"I'm not sure. Every time they talked tactics, they locked me in a closet and spoke Korean so I couldn't understand anyway. But I don't think it will be many. Shin prides himself on doing things the smart way. Quick, easy, in and out." Strange pointed to the side of his head. "And with some tricks. But when he talked strategy, the big picture, Shin did confide in me." Strange grinned broadly, proud to have some inside information that we didn't have.

When Strange didn't elaborate, Ernie finally said, "Good. Just keep quiet about it." He rummaged through the pockets of his field jacket. "Sueño, where did I leave those brass knuckles?"

"They have to be in there somewhere," I said. "You never leave home without them."

Strange reached out and touched Ernie's elbow. "Wait. What are you doing?"

"I'm going to beat the *strategy* information out of you. A helluva lot more fun than begging you to share."

"Hold on," Strange replied. "I was going to tell you."

Ernie's face reddened. "Then goddam *tell* us! Now!"

"Okay. Keep your fatigue shirt on."

Strange laid out the broad strokes of what Shin was up to. Apparently, the Great Leader was sick and tired of standing by while blood-sucking American imperialists exploited South Korea's workers and turned all their women into harlots. It was time to liberate the South. But because of the combined strength of the American-supported South Korean Army and the air, naval, and ground strength of the US forces, an extra factor had to be brought to bear.

"The Russians?" Ernie asked.

"No," Strange replied. "According to the Great Leader, the Soviets have grown soft, lost their revolutionary zeal. So have the Chinese, and, besides, the North Koreans don't trust the Chinese. They've invaded Korea too many times."

In ancient history, dozens of times.

"So who's going to help?" Ernie asked.

"The people of South Korea themselves. The rural proletariat, the Great Leader calls them."

I knew "rural proletariat" to be a contradiction in terms but didn't interrupt. Ernie and I were both listening in rapt attention and therefore Strange was wallowing in his happy space.

"The plan is to first push back this Marine Corps landing. That will provide plenty of publicity worldwide and show the people of South Korea that the US is not invincible. Then commandos on fast-moving boats will be flooded in to conquer the East Coast. The entire range called the Taebaek Mountains. From Pohang up to the DMZ. The farmers and miners and hunters who live there are rugged, independent people. If they take up arms and join the revolutionary vanguard of the Great Leader, a long-term guerilla war can be waged, and although the South Korean puppet government, according to Shin, might never surrender, it is thought the Americans will quickly back away from such a conflict."

"Because we learned our lesson in Vietnam," Ernie said.

"Exactly. It is fresh in the minds of the American public and there will be no support for waging more endless combat in Asia."

"In other words," I said, "this Mr. Shin is planning on starting a war."

Strange grabbed his cigarette holder and blew on it like a whistle, pretending to clean it. And then he said, "Right. Shin expects Yoon-ah to help him."

We all pondered that as we drove a couple of more klicks toward Namho. Finally, Ernie spoke, "What's this Yoon-ah, as you call her, going to do against a battalion of US Marines?"

When Strange didn't answer, I said, "It's not what she'll do to them. It has to do with the 'trick' Shin is setting up."

"What trick?"

We both looked at Strange. He looked befuddled and said, "*Moolah* the hell out of me."

When the road churned upward, Ernie found a turnoff and parked the jeep beside a clump of bushes. We climbed out. Pushing branches out of the way, we gazed up to the top of the ridge and could just make out some sort of military emplacement. Camouflage netting was draped over what might have been an armored vehicle. Soldiers milled about on either side of a narrow road.

"That's it," Ernie said. "The final checkpoint. Strange and I will continue on in the jeep."

"The name's Harvey," Strange said.

"Whatever. Sueño, you're going to have to climb over that mountain ridge, keeping your distance from that checkpoint. Meet us on the other side."

"And don't get spotted by any ROK Army patrols," Strange added.

"He already *knows* that, Bozo," Ernie told him.

"Who you calling Bozo?"

"You see any other clowns around here?"

I told them to calm down. I'd walk over the ridge. In the fading sunlight, I studied its contours. "Over there," I said, pointing. "It looks like a saddle between two humps in the ridge."

"Yeah. I see it. We'll set up a position on the other side and wait for you."

"It'll be dark," I said. "How will I find you? The ROK Army's not going to allow any lights, not just hours before such an important operation."

Ernie and Strange looked at one another. Finally, Ernie said, "If we can, we'll park near a hut or a farmhouse or any sort of structure directly downhill from that saddle. No idea what's there, if anything, but that's where we'll wait. Unless there's no cover. If we're just sitting out there prior to the landing, somebody's bound to come by and start asking questions."

"Tell them you're CID," I said. "With important information concerning security."

"If I do that, they'll take us away to wherever the command post is."

"That'll be okay," I said. "If I can't find you, I'll know you had to move. The main thing is that we find Shin and make sure he doesn't disrupt the landing."

"Don't forget Miss Kim," Strange added.

"Will you quit worrying about her?" Ernie said. "I'm more worried about them destroying equipment, like they did with the pontoons or, God forbid, murdering a few US Marines and starting a war. One North Korean turncoat doesn't concern me all that much."

"Well, it ought to." Strange started to pout.

That was enough of their bickering for me. "There's a pear orchard over there," I said. "Before it gets too dark, I'm going to walk through there, then up and over the ridge."

"One more thing." Ernie rummaged through the emergency equipment kit he kept stowed beneath the front passenger seat. He grabbed what he wanted and handed it to me. "You'll need this," he said.

A flashlight. I stuck it in my back pocket. "Thanks."

Without further ceremony, I climbed an old wooden fence and marched toward the pear orchard.

The pears were too green to eat. Suddenly, I thought it would've been nice if we'd thought to bring some C rations. Or even if I had some money in my pocket to buy a packet of instant noodles somewhere. I was so hungry I could suck on them dry. That was, if I ever reached civilization again.

The orchard was behind me now, the terrain rocky and filled with weeds and wild grass. I reminded myself that the Koreans liked to claim that there were no snakes in their country, but I wasn't sure it was true. Maybe no poisonous ones, I hoped, but everyone had snakes, didn't they? They had to be one of the oldest animals.

I shoved snakes out of my mind and thought about Kim Yoon-jeong, the North Korean woman. Whose side was she on? Probably, I imagined, just her own and her children's. Or was she an opportunist and dangerous? Who knew what connections she had in governments on either side of the DMZ? And she'd proven herself to be disdainful of the law, enticing Strange into violating his oath of enlistment for her. Turning him into, in effect, a traitor. Had I gone too far as well? How compromised was I at this point? We'd been so focused on stopping the attacks on Focus Lens that I hadn't given much thought to my own precarious legal position, not so much because I didn't have time, but more because I didn't want to face facts. I could end up losing my military career, the only gainful employment I'd ever had, and end up with not only a DD, a dishonorable discharge, but also a few years—or even decades—of staring at four cement walls in a federal prison.

While these thoughts ran through my mind, I'd made a lot of progress up the side of the ridge, but there wasn't much of a moon, and I was groping around like a blind man now. I grabbed the flashlight Ernie had given me, switched it on, and aimed it at the ground.

Nothing.

I opened it and jiggled the batteries around, but still nothing.

Angrily, I tossed it away.

Apparently Ernie's arrangement with the head dispatcher of the 21st Transportation Company didn't cover batteries.

When I reached the top of the ridge, I looked down. Just a few small lights glimmering here and there. Beyond, was what seemed to be a flat expanse, then the sound of waves rolling in. The perfect place to land an invading force. But also the perfect place to situate a machine-gun emplacement to mow them down.

I started moving downhill very carefully. The decline was steep enough that it would've been dangerous in the light of day. At night it was treacherous, and I didn't want to break a leg or crack my head open. So it took me hours, almost until dawn to reach the lowlands. Exhausted, I sat and watched the sun rise out of the Eastern Sea. *Outer Japan 'crost the Bay*, as Rudyard Kipling might've said if he'd been in similar circumstances.

Almost a mile off to the left I spotted a short line of GP tents, one of them with a red cross printed on a white background. The one in the center was probably the logistical headquarters. A communications truck was parked next to it, antennas reaching skyward. And then a couple of more tents. GIs drove up in a three-quarter-ton truck and unloaded folding tables and what looked like coffee or hot water urns. Probably where the press corps would be greeted.

No sign of Ernie or Strange. They might've gotten waylaid

at the main checkpoint. For all I knew, they'd been taken into custody and were languishing in a lockup somewhere.

But what intrigued me most was the thatched-roof farmhouse below. Behind it was a smaller building with a brown ox tethered out front. A pile of hay had been thrust in front of the creature, and I guessed the bovine had been coaxed out of its tiny shelter in order to make room for someone, or something, else.

I was right.

While I waited, a soldier emerged from the front of the tiny barn. Or was it a soldier? Wearing fatigues, yes, but too much hair piled atop the head. And then I realized what I was looking at. A husky redheaded woman I'd seen before. A woman who'd pointed a pistol at me at Camp Long and then fought by my side at the bivouac area next to the Pyeongchang River. Corporal Hurley. She was with another female soldier and a woman wearing khaki pants and a khaki jungle jacket with a canvas bag slung over her shoulder. Katie Byrd Worthington.

My shock was mingled with delight. *What were they doing here?* Whatever their reason, I was happy they'd arrived. Clearly, the party could now officially start.

An hour later, three green army buses rolled up to the line of GP tents on the far end of the beach. Civilians with various types of recording equipment emerged single file, and then

TV cameras were unloaded from trapdoors in the back of the buses.

Off the coast, the early morning mist lifted, revealing an amphibious attack ship hovering about a mile offshore. Soon, like drones born from a queen, smaller landing craft were spontaneously generated, and a phalanx of them buzzed toward the shoreline. The surf was relatively calm, breakers only about four feet high at their worst, and the landing craft navigated the swells easily. Finally, the first boat hit the beach. The front ramp lowered, and marines in full combat gear sprinted off, sloshing through white foam. After a few yards, they slammed themselves onto sand and aimed their assault rifles and machine guns forward, providing cover for the marines following closely behind. Almost immediately, four or five other craft hit the beach, and soon there was a formidable force of combatants crawling inland, pretending occasionally to engage an enemy. Using blanks, the invading marauders popped off a few rounds, giving the entire morning the illusion of verisimilitude.

The TV cameras were rolling, the announcers jawboning into mics, and Katie Byrd Worthington scurried around like a beetle beneath a spotlight, kneeling occasionally, snapping pictures, and clicking new flashbulbs into her camera's holder.

While everyone concentrated on the drama of the landing, a convoy of three wooden carts rolled along the main road descending from the ridge, heading toward the line of green army buses. The people pushing the carts were wearing the hemp garments of poor Korean farmers. The carts probably contained what I was most longing for, instant noodles ready for boiling and maybe some dried cuttlefish and plastic-wrapped Choco Pies—marshmallow crusted with a layer of cheap chocolate—and almost certainly plenty of Fanta Orange and bottle after bottle of Korean-made crystalline soju.

The American Marines were stationed in Okinawa, and on this visit, they would be introduced to their first taste of Korean cuisine.

I turned back to the action on the beach and noticed that some of the reporters had now ventured forward and were holding microphones in front of the marines. Their officers were allowing them to speak, although you could bet they'd been briefed on what they were allowed to say. This was all seen as great propaganda for the military alliance between the United States and South Korea, an alliance that kept the vicious forces of the Great Leader, Kim Il-sung, firmly on his side of the DMZ.

Even Katie Byrd was talking to some of the marines, listening and jotting down notes.

Corporal Hurley and the other female soldiers had kept well back from the main action, although they were all dressed in full combat gear, had their M16 rifles at the ready, and seemed prepared for just about anything.

One of the vendors at the last cart knelt down, and I figured

he was about to bring out one of the wooden cases of glistening green bottles of soju. Instead, he stayed low, fiddling with
something that was out of my sight. What I did notice was that
he raised something until it barely peeked over the top of the
cart like a coat hanger.

And then I realized what it was. An antenna.

-19-

A field radio had been hidden in that cart.

I strained to see his face. Was it Mr. Shin? From this distance, I couldn't be sure. I looked again at the woman with a hemp tunic, her hood pulled over her head. When she stood up to pile more ramen packets atop the cart, even through the thick material, I recognized the elegant proportions of her figure. Kim Yoon-jeong.

Why was she here? She wasn't a combatant. But when it came to distraction she could do plenty of that when she put her mind to it. She'd certainly caused plenty of distraction in the Hamilton Hotel Coffee Shop. But out here, the distraction would be used to smuggle that radio past the military guards who were supposed to search the carts thoroughly. And if, as I suspected, the man operating the radio equipment was Shin, him having a woman posing as his wife would make it seem as if they were simply a local mom-and-pop operation trying to make a few extra bucks while a group of rich American GIs had been dropped into their midst.

I looked down at where Hurley and her comrades were waiting. Apparently, Katie Byrd had brought them here. Why? What did she suspect? It didn't matter now. The point was that they were here and I needed them. I rose from my hiding place and started running downhill, slowing only to make sure I didn't lose my footing and tumble forward and break my neck. As I ran, I glanced at the man I presumed was Mr. Shin. He was bent over, talking rapidly, not at a person but into the radio.

When I approached the women at the tiny oxen barn, they turned to look at the crazy man running toward them, waving his arms. Corporal Hurley stood, threw her cigarette into the sand, and stubbed it out with the toe of her combat boot.

"Sueño," she said when I reached her. "What the hell are you doing here?"

I pointed, still breathless. "The buses," I gasped out. "Behind them. Three carts. One of them has a radio in it."

Hurley turned and looked. She reached down, grabbed her helmet, slipped it on, and tightened the leather strap beneath her chin. "Come on," she said to the women around her. They all jumped to their feet and grabbed their rifles. As they formed up and started to move out toward the carts, something whistled overhead. A high, keening sound, very much, I imagined, like death.

The sound came closer and then hit with an impact that

caused us all to leap toward the ground. Hurley was the first back on her feet. "Move!" she shouted, and the war women began running, as one, toward the three carts.

More rounds fell. Mortar shells. The explosions first hitting uselessly on the beach, but then moving steadily toward the marines. Whoever was working that radio was communicating with the mortar platoon somewhere in the mountains, or on the far side of them, outside the defensive perimeter set up by the ROK Army. And the guy with the radio was guiding their fire toward the target.

The Marine Corps doctrine is that when you're under fire, the best defense is to attack. The problem was that these rounds were indirect fire, raining in from the sky. Still, their leaders shouted commands and moved forward, some of them right into the barrage of explosions, but most of them soon made their way toward the shelter of the tumbled boulders that were concentrated just where the terrain began to rise.

Meanwhile, Corporal Hurley and her soldiers had almost reached the three wooden carts when someone opened fire on them. Automatic fire. Withering. I was running after them, tugging on the waistline of my beltless pants, when the rounds started coming toward us. I fell to the ground, as did everyone else. Without being told, the women returned fire, and under that cover, Hurley rose to her feet and moved out, heading directly for whoever was wielding the automatic rifle. It sounded again. Hurley stopped running and, for the briefest moment, stood still, as if frozen in a forward crouch. Slowly she rolled forward, falling into the sand in a face-first dive.

This enflamed the rest of the war women. Again, without orders, they rose to their feet and moved forward, walking this time, but laying down a relentless wall of fire, some of them reaching into their ammo pouches and replacing magazines, rolling forward as a unit across the last few yards of beach like a catastrophic tornado crossing the plains of Oklahoma.

One or two of them went down, but within seconds the lead women had overrun the carts and began taking whoever was still alive into custody.

The officer in charge of the Marine Corps Expeditionary Force ran up behind me. His nametag said Wallace. His rank was captain.

"What in the hell?" he asked.

I shook my head. "Sabotage," I said.

We both looked up at the sound of choppers flying overhead. The ominous machines zoomed past us, low, heading for the far side of the ridge.

"ROK Army," I told him. "They've already zeroed in on whoever was firing those mortars."

"What are they going to do with them?" he asked.

"They'll be dead within minutes," I said, "if not less."

Explosions sounded on the far side of the ridge, and shortly thereafter smoke rose in the distance, caressing the jagged edges of the craggy peaks.

I walked forward and examined the guts of the radio lying near the cart, tubes and wires smashed by a rifle round. Next to the radio, in the hemp garments of a medieval peasant farmer, lay the man I knew as Mr. Shin. His eyes stared lifelessly up at the sky, but the Seiko watch on his wrist kept on ticking. Two more men in hemp lay dead, one of them with an AK-47 automatic rifle still grasped in his hand. I wondered if these had been the guys who'd attacked us in Itaewon near the *nakji* house. The woman at the front cart was still breathing but wounded. I reached down and pulled back her hood.

The Widow Kim, the stunning beauty from North Korea, stared up at me. "I had to do it," she told me. "I had no choice. My children."

I let go of her and stepped away. Her eyes held mine as a bevy of army medics surrounded her, two or three of them kneeling and checking on the men I already knew to be dead.

I walked away from the blood and the carnage. The war women were gathered around Corporal Hurley, some of them kneeling, covering their eyes with their free hand and gripping their M16 rifles pointed at the sky with the other. A medic pressed his fingers deep into the side of Hurley's neck, but finally he shook his head and stood up and walked over toward his fellows. The women did their best to stifle their tears, but as brave as they were, they weren't able to do so.

Neither was I.

-20-

Ernie and Strange had been taken into custody at the MP checkpoint and been shackled all night in the back of a three-quarter-ton truck, the military equivalent of a paddy wagon. When they were finally released, Ernie found me and said, "What in the hell happened to you?"

Katie Byrd Worthington sat next to me on a wooden bench that had been set up near the Command Post GP tent. She was scribbling furiously into her notebook.

Strange, standing behind Ernie, looked around anxiously.

"The medics took your girlfriend to a hospital near Pohang," I told him. "She's only wounded."

For once he didn't quibble about the designation "girl-friend."

"What's the name of the hospital?" he asked.

"Don't even," Katie Byrd said, still writing on the pad propped on her knee. "As we speak, the KNPs have her under arrest. The best thing you can do for her is hire a good lawyer."

Ernie noticed the military coroner's van.

"Who is it?" he asked.

"Mr. Shin," I said. "And a couple of his thugs."

"That's the civilian body count," Katie added. "They've finally been cleared away. It took the army forever to get that van out here. The bodies have just been lying in the sand, covered by ponchos."

"Who else?" Ernie asked again.

"Two marines," I said. "The wounded have already been airlifted out."

"Christ," Ernie said. "That's it?"

I looked at Katie. She stopped writing and stared directly at Ernie. "One more," she said. "Not a Marine but a soldier. US Army. Transportation Corps. You know her."

"*Her?*" Ernie asked.

Katie Byrd glanced down at her notes. "Corporal Phyllis A. Hurley, late of the 877th Field Transportation Company."

In the silence, I asked the question I'd been wanting to ask. "Why, Katie? Why did you all come here?"

She took a deep breath and started to talk. "After that barbaric display at Camp Long, the gals were pretty down in the dumps, especially Phyllis. Maybe I shouldn't have done it, but I told them about this amphibious landing this morning and how you guys were worried there might be trouble. Phyllis was on it first. She wanted to go. Some of the others were worried about being charged with AWOL along with their other problems, but in the end they decided to grab their three-quarter-ton truck and make it over here to help in any way they could. We drove up here, and once we talked our way past the ROK Army checkpoints, we paid a farmer to let us hide in his barn, leaving his prize ox out in the cold all night. And then we stood by, waiting for the Marine Corps to arrive."

It made sense that the ROK Army wouldn't have stopped them. They were looking for North Korean commandos, not a unit of American females.

"She died a hero," Katie said, staring down at her notebook.

For once, Ernie agreed with her.

Katie kept staring at her notebook for a long time, until finally she dog-eared a page and folded it shut.

-21-

At the trial of Kim Yoon-jeong, Strange testified as a character witness. He told the judge and a courtroom jammed to the rafters that he'd met her during a talk she and some other North Korean escapees had given to ROK and US intelligence analysts. Cross-examined about exactly how that occurred, he admitted that she'd initiated the contact during punch and cookies after the event, slipping a piece of paper into his hand with a date and time on it and a place for them to meet: the Hamilton Hotel Coffee Shop.

Soon after, he'd been introduced to her mother and her three children, and before he really had time to absorb his good luck, he was purchasing her small items out of the commissary and PX. She eventually invited him to move in with her. They had indeed listened clandestinely to prohibited evening North Korean radio broadcasts, but he claimed that instead of trying to propagandize him, she spent most of the time explaining how many lies the announcer was spouting.

One after the other, she said. North Korea wasn't a worker's paradise, but a place of fear and misery and the country best known for the enslavement of an entire people.

When asked why he'd stolen the classified document concerning unit deployments during the Focus Lens joint exercise, Strange admitted he'd been blinded by love. And by fear. He saw it in her eyes when her son was taken by the North Korean agents, and neither one of them had any doubt that Mr. Shin and his cohorts would show no mercy.

Kim Yoon-jeong herself, when she took the stand, apologized profusely to the people of South Korea, to Sergeant Harvey for getting him in so much trouble, and especially to the families of the servicemen, both Korean and American, who'd been hurt or killed by the North Korean commandos. She admitted that she deserved punishment but pleaded with the court for understanding.

"I only feared for the life of my son," she told them, "and later for the lives of my mother and for the lives of all my children. Not for my own life. I would've gladly died rather than betray the country that has so generously granted me refuge."

In the end, she was sentenced to twenty-five years for treason against the Republic of Korea. Of that, she would serve only five years in prison, followed by twenty years of indentured service in the form of projects to be assigned by the Ministry of Defense, at a time and place of their choosing. This meant that she would be a spy for South Korea. Beholden to them now, after being so sorely used by their Communist counterparts.

Graciously, the Widow Kim Yoon-jeong bowed to the court and thanked the judge for his empathy.

Strange, like all of us, was considered for a commendation for his action in attempting to thwart the North Korean commando attack on the amphibious landing operation. This was balanced, however, by his egregious unauthorized release of classified documents. In the end, 8th Army JAG decided to drop the entire issue. No charges against Strange, since he'd been coerced by North Korean agents into stealing the documents and had the welfare of innocent civilians at heart. He would, however, receive "specialized training" on what to do if approached by a foreign agent. Another way of saying that he was going to have to work a hellacious amount of overtime from now until Major Cranston grew weary of seeing him around the office.

Ernie and I were chewed out royally by Colonel Brace at about the same time, and in the same breath, as we were commended by him for helping save as many marines as we had. The embarrassment of the ludicrous charges brought against us by Burrows and Slabem was not mentioned. Staff Sergeant Riley later told us that the honchos realized that I had only checked out the classified document to use as bait to entice the network of North Korean spies, and I had never actually turned it over to them. Quietly, the charges were dropped.

Embarrassment—for wild *kisaeng* parties, missing classified documents, botched amphibious landings—was a powerful incentive for the US military to shun publicity. And courts-martial and newspaper articles and letters to congressmen attracted embarrassment like rotting meat attracts flies. So Ernie and I, after our butt-chewing by Colonel Brace, were put back on the black-market detail, told this time to stick strictly to over-purchases of bananas and Spam and maraschino cherries. Things we were qualified to handle.

What really hurt was what happened to the war women.

-22-

Katie Byrd Worthington met us at a subterranean bistro in Myong-dong, the downtown Seoul party and shopping district whose name literally meant the Bright District. It was a bohemian spot with a guy in the corner strumming on a mandolin, tables with checkered tablecloths and guttering candles, and a list of imported Italian wines that cost way more than Ernie and I were willing to pay.

"Not to worry," Katie said when she saw us gawking at the price list. "They have draft OB."

And so Ernie and I each ordered a large mug of Oriental Beer while Katie ordered a glass of something hard to pronounce, and we were glad to see that she was buying.

"I want to thank you guys for your help," she said.

"Knock off the bullshit, Katie," Ernie told her. "What do you want?"

She shook her head until her short-cropped hair rustled. "Nothing. You got me all wrong. Those gals at the transportation unit really touched me." She sipped on her glass of vino. "Especially Hurley."

We raised our drinks and clicked them together. "Here's to Corporal Phyllis A. Hurley," I said. "A true hero."

"Hear! Hear!"

We waited. The guy strumming the mandolin finished what he was playing, and a young woman with a violin took his place.

"They're going to transfer them all out," Katie said. "Back to the States. Maybe one or two will be sent to Europe. They want to break them up, isolate their stories, make them less effective as a team."

"But your articles made a hell of an impact," I said. "The Associated Press picked them up, and plenty of stateside papers ran the story too. Congress even got involved and forced Eighth Army to start an investigation into the death of Helen Ochs."

The issue had been seen as so serious back in DC that instead of the army doing the investigating, a small team of FBI agents had been flown into Korea. Oddly, they didn't interview me or Ernie. But they had put Staff Sergeant "Mule" Skinner through the wringer, and he and two of his buddies admitted to the assault and rape of Private Helen Ochs, although they denied having anything to do with her death. It did appear to be a suicide. They'd already been shipped back to the States and would be serving their time for assault and rape at the federal penitentiary in Leavenworth, Kansas. A fourth member of the gang was still holding out, his parents' being wealthy enough to hire him a fancy lawyer. Still, word was that he'd go down eventually, just with a lighter sentence than the others—money meaning what it does in American jurisprudence.

"I guess you're right," Katie said, looking back and forth between us. "We did some good, didn't we?"

I nodded. "But it was mostly them. They're the ones who blew the whistle. They're the ones who insisted on being treated fairly. They're the ones who put it all on the line."

She stared back into her wine. "Sometimes I wonder, what's the point?"

Ernie patted her on the back. "Don't give up, Katie Byrd. You're the best."

She studied him. "You really think so?"

"Absolutely." He quaffed down more beer.

Katie sat up straighter. "Good. Then I've got another one for you. This gal down in Pusan. She works for the signal unit down there—"

"*Whoa*," Ernie said, raising his hands. "We've been read the riot act. Black-market detail *only*."

Katie Byrd frowned and scrunched her nose. "You gonna wimp out on me, Bascom?"

"Wimp out?"

"That's what I said."

"Of course not," he replied.

"Then here's her name." She slid a stack of paperwork toward the center of the table. Ernie stared at it as if it were hazardous nuclear waste. I set my beer down, reached out, and picked it up. Twisting the top sheet to catch the dim candlelight, I said, "Do you have photos?"

"Wouldn't come to you without 'em," Katie Byrd replied, patting her canvas bag.

"Well then," I said. "Looks like we're back in business."

Ernie groaned.

Katie called the violin player over. As she stood there holding her instrument and her bow, Katie Byrd asked her if she knew "Jambalaya."

When the violinist looked at me blankly, I hesitated, wondering how to translate that. Instead, the three of us just started to sing it. The violin player recognized the song and she was soon fiddling like a Cajun. The other customers in the joint, and even the waitstaff, started clapping their hands, some of them knowing the words and belting them out as lustily as me and Ernie.

As the tune reverberated through the little room, Katie Byrd pulled out her notebook, thumbed to the dog-eared page, underlined the name Phyllis A. Hurley, and stared at it for a long time.